THE LIES OF THE AJUNGO

THE LIES OF THE
AJUNGO

MOSES OSE UTOMI

TOR PUBLISHING GROUP
NEW YORK

THE LIES OF THE AJUNGO

A Tordotcom Book
Published by Tom Doherty Associates/Tor Publishing Group
120 Broadway
New York, NY 10271

www.tor.com

Tor® is a registered trademark of Macmillan Publishing Group, LLC.

Library of Congress Cataloging-in-Publication Data

Names: Utomi, Moses Ose, author.
Title: The lies of the Ajungo / Moses Ose Utomi.
Description: First edition. | New York : Tordotcom, A Tom Doherty
Associates Book, 2023. | Series: The forever desert; 1
Identifiers: LCCN 2022041374 (print) | LCCN 2022041375 (ebook) |
ISBN 9781250849069 (hardcover) | ISBN 9781250848420 (ebook)
Subjects: LCGFT: Novellas.
Classification: LCC PS3621.T66 L54 2023 (print) |
LCC PS3621.T66 (ebook) | DDC 813/.6—dc23
LC record available at https://lccn.loc.gov/2022041374
LC ebook record available at https://lccn.loc.gov/2022041375

Our books may be purchased in bulk for promotional,
educational, or business use. Please contact the Macmillan Corporate
and Premium Sales Department at 1-800-221-7945, extension 5442,
or by email at MacmillanSpecialMarkets@macmillan.com.

First Edition: 2023

Printed in the United States of America

0 9 8 7 6 5 4 3 2 1

To my parents,
Oseyi Mike Utomi and Stella Odalomhen Uwaibi-Utomi,
who journeyed bravely beyond their City of Lies,
shared generously the water they found,
and prepared me for my own journey
through the Forever Desert.

THE LIES OF THE AJUNGO

1

THERE IS NO WATER in the *City of Lies*.

There hasn't been for as long as any can remember. The Great-mamas tell stories about the Fever, when not a single cloud was seen for years and even the cacti puckered and died. Breezes became natural disasters, stirring up enough fine, choked sand to blind the city for days. Mamas drank the blood of their children to fend off thirst, only to die anyway; too late they learned that blood was no substitute.

To the north, the Ajungo Empire had water like sky. They drank their fill, bathed daily, planted seeds and watched them grow into trees fat with fruit. Orulu, oba of the City of Lies, pleaded with the Ajungo for aid, but the Ajungo were sworn to selfishness. In exchange for water, the Ajungo demanded the tongues of every citizen of the City of Lies. It was a twofold price, a price of blood and a price of history: an untongued people cannot tell their story.

But neither can the dead.

So Orulu paid the price. All the city's citizens—everyone thirteen years and older—had their tongues cut away by hot blades, dumped into wagons, and shipped across the continent. In exchange, water was given, but not enough for the city to recover. Only a trickle. Just enough to keep the people of the City of Lies alive. Just enough to make it worth the price.

That was when the Ajungo renamed the city. Those old enough to remember the city's original name had no tongues to speak, and those young enough to speak had no memory.

Orulu himself, still in his youth, undertook a journey. He left with a promise to return a hero. He would traverse the Forever

Desert—braving its scorching heat, monstrous beasts, and roaming Ajungo killers—in hopes of finding another people that could come to their aid. But when he finally found another empire and told them of the Ajungo's betrayal, they did not believe; who would trust the leader of a city named for deceit?

So Orulu returned, but he was no hero.

There are no heroes in the City of Lies.

Generation after generation, Orulu watched from the high towers of the Palace of Lies as wagons were loaded with the tongues of his people. Eventually, in his final years, he assembled his people for an emergency address. They gathered in the town square, a wide expanse that had long ago been a beautiful field where children had played and adults had napped, heads laid against soft grass. Now it was just low dunes of ankle-deep sand that scorched the nose with each breath.

Looking upon his weak, dehydrated people, Orulu made a plea. He called on the city's children, those young enough to still have their tongues. He besought them to roam wide and far, to find a new land with water, where they could build a new city, begin a new history.

It would only take one, he told them. Not an act of heroism, but a stroke of luck. One child who could stumble into the right valley or come across a friendly face. Even a child deemed a liar could find someone to trust her, Orulu believed.

Hundreds of years passed. Orulu and his daughter and his daughter's daughter all ruled and died and no water was ever found. Children left, but none returned. For most, the task was simply too much. Beyond the city walls, the Forever Desert was as dry and unforgiving as a dead man's heart—no place for a child. For others, the quest was a selfish one, a chance to escape the drought and tongue-cutting that awaited them at home, to find a new land where they could live. In either case, children were lost, never to be seen again.

And all came to understand: *There are no friends beyond the City of Lies.*

Soon those children who proclaimed they would attempt the royal quest and seek out water came to be viewed with both pity and suspicion. Everyone knew they would fail, and they did by the thousands. Big and small, clever and foolish, in the heat of day and the chill of night, each child was lost to the Forever Desert, never to return.

Then there was Tutu.

*   *   *

Tutu had never liked school.

Not because of the teachers or the lessons—within the walls of their one-room schoolhouse, where Madam Oda taught history and math and science, he felt peace. But before class and after, when it was just him and the other students, he struggled to remember why he came to this horrible place.

You must learn. He could see his mama's fingers signing in his memory. *Only by learning can you free us.*

"Tutu, how is your mouth?" his classmates asked in near unison, giggling.

They'd been asking the same question every morning for weeks.

"It is fine," he said, keeping his eyes ahead. He just had to weather their taunts until Madam Oda arrived.

"Your tongue does not hurt?"

Though he was smaller than his classmates, he was a year older. In three days it would be his thirteenth birthday, which meant he would be cut. His mouth felt cold at the thought of it, and an uneasiness swam in his stomach. It was scary, of course, to think of the pain. Or to think he would never taste his mama's cooking again. But it was scariest of all to think that he hadn't learned enough. In three days he'd be tongueless, removed from school and put to work mining iron or at some other such labor.

He couldn't even free himself, much less the whole city.

"If your tongue hurts, we can cut it for you."

"It is fine," he repeated. Madam Oda had never been this late. Something was wrong.

"Will you cry when they cut you, Tutu?"

"How much blood do you think you will make?"

"Maybe your tongue will get infected and you will die."

"Will you cry?"

"Cry, cry, cry!"

He knew how much they wanted him to cry, but he always denied them. *Tears are precious*, his mama always said. *Don't waste them on your enemies. Save them for your friends.*

Still, Tutu's eyes were beginning to sting and the first tears were clouding together when Madam Oda swept into the room, her normally serene eyes panicked, her thin cheeks even more sunken than usual.

Tutu! she signed, the shaking in her fingers conveying meaning enough. *You must go.*

His classmates hushed. Tutu looked at her, confused. "Why, Madam?"

Your mama.

*   *   *

Outside Tutu's square, sheet iron home, the neighbors stood in a somber half circle.

"Mama?" he called.

As each person in the crowd became aware of his presence, they turned to look at him, pity plain on their faces. They parted for his approach, revealing his mama splayed out on the desert floor. She was brushed in sand, as if she'd been there long enough for the wind to start burying her. Her eyes were closed.

Tutu walked carefully toward her, telling himself that she was only pretending. But when he knelt beside her and saw that her lips were bone dry, her cheeks sharp and bloodless, her eyelids so thin that her veins bulged all along them, he knew the truth. It was dehydration. "Blood drought."

He looked around at his neighbors, at their drawn faces and taut skin. Their swollen ribcages and bent backs. He understood why they'd left her lying there. The drought had been bad for the last week, and many of them were especially weak. When water was low and thirst was high, it was risky to waste energy helping others.

He understood. But he hated them all the same.

The taunts of his classmates had only ever made him feel sad. Lonely. This made him feel angry. An anger so dark and miserable that he froze as it passed through him, not sure what would happen if he moved.

"Tutu . . ." someone said in a calm, comforting voice.

But he ignored it. The only thing he wanted from any of them was for them to help his mama. But they'd refused. They'd made it clear that they didn't love him or his mama. That if he didn't protect her, no one else would.

He dragged his mama out from under the sun and their neighbors' pitying gazes and into their cramped one-room home. Even without help, and even as small as he was, his mama had lost so much weight that it wasn't difficult for him to sit her up against the back wall. From the coolest corner of their house, he retrieved their iron saucer of water. He knew she had chosen to pass out and save the water for him rather than drink it herself, but he refused to watch her grip on life slip away.

Tutu tilted his mama's head back, tapped her jaw down, and dribbled a bit of water over her lips and onto her tongue. He watched as the moisture seeped away, then he continued trickling the water in until her eyes fluttered open and rolled in delirium.

Their meager water was almost finished. It wouldn't last another day, and there was no guarantee of when more would come.

His mama wouldn't be the first person to die of thirst in the City of Lies.

He had to get more.

He could try to steal some from his neighbors. They all owed his mama for what they'd done. But he'd never been quick nor sneaky, and if he got caught, he would be beaten, maybe even jailed—neither of which would help her.

He could beg. Maybe if a ration of water had been distributed recently, someone would have shared, but not now.

He could search for it himself, dig around the city for any hidden wells that had yet to be tapped. But he had no idea how to do that, and, of course, *there is no water in the City of Lies.*

Most importantly, none of those would change anything. If he stole water now, he would need to steal more the next time. If a neighbor shared some with him now, would he be back at their door in a month, begging? If he managed to find the first wet well in centuries, how much water could he get before everyone else swooped in to claim their own share?

This was no way to live—from drought to drought, praying the body would survive this one, only to pray again when the next one came. He had to make a change, and he didn't have much time. Soon, he wouldn't have a tongue.

"Mama, I must go," he said softly. "I must find water."

He'd thought about it for years. He'd even once mentioned it to his classmates at the schoolhouse, only to meet ridicule. Since then, he'd kept his plan to himself, thinking it over and over, discarding it just to have it scuttle back to the front of his mind like a determined scorpion.

There are no heroes in the City of Lies.

His mama's eyes unglued and she stared at him in near recognition. He raised the saucer again to her lips to give her the rest of the water before he left, but her hand shot up to grip his wrist, stunningly strong.

"Mama?"

Her neck rotated one way, then the other: a slow, arduous *no*. She moved his wrist toward his own mouth. At first he resisted, but when he saw how much strength it was taking from her shaking arm, he allowed her to put the saucer to his lips. He even tilted his head back and let her pour the last trickle of sacred water down his throat.

He felt tears building behind his eyes, but he squinted them back, refusing to cry in front of her.

Tears are precious, he could imagine her signing.

Summoning the last of her energy, veins straining against the skin of her throat, his mama leaned forward and kissed him on the forehead. Her lips were so dry and brittle that they scratched his skin. She issued a prayer, her throat rasping with the memory of speech, the stump of her tongue wiggling, feeble and ineffective.

Then she closed her eyes and collapsed back against the wall.

He smoothed her hair. It was wet from sweat, but he knew that sweat was old. Soon, it would dry up just like everything else did. He'd seen so many arid corpses in his short life, sprawled in the city's desert streets like any other fallen animal. His brothers and sisters had all suffered that fate. After watching helplessly as child after child succumbed to blood drought, his mama had done everything in her power and beyond to keep Tutu, her last, watered. Now it was his turn to pay her back.

With nothing but his mama's blessing and the threadbare leather sandals on his feet, he left his home. There was no water in the City of Lies, true, but he would prove that there was a hero in the City of Lies.

At least one.

*   *   *

The Palace of Lies was a towering, pointed structure built atop a round plateau near the city walls. All around its base and on the edges of its high window slits, emerald and ruby and sapphire tiles were laid in glittering patterns and gradients. The rest of it was covered in wooden pilasters that jutted a stride out from its exterior walls. The brown alabaster stairs up to its doors were high enough that as Tutu reached the top whistling winds tugged at him. He looked back at the city and saw that his entire neighborhood was an indistinguishable plot of squat homes among the red sand. He couldn't pick out his own house.

Upon entering the throne room, he was greeted by a checkered floor of black-and-white squares and a ceiling ten times higher than the tallest man, with a mesmerizing symmetry of color tiled into it.

Before him, at the back of the room, sat Oba Ijefi. Her glistening curls spiraled outward in a thick white cloud. She was wrapped in fine silk, as crimson as blood. Dangling webs of gold glittered at her neck and wrists. Her throne was a rich red-black wood, curved so perfectly for her body it looked like the tree had grown around her.

Tutu had never seen wood before, but it looked like how he imagined from the stories. It was imbued with life, the most ancient skin—its knots like eyes, its folds like wetted lips, breathing into him from across the room. It was the cleanest thing he'd ever smelled.

The royal court fanned out on both sides of the oba on her throne—family and guards and advisers. They stood at attention, swathed in the same red silks, mouths hidden behind bronze half-masks etched with flowing shapes Tutu didn't recognize.

Tutu prostrated himself, forehead against the checkered floor, arms crossed over his chest.

"Rise, Speaker," said Oba Ijefi. She was the only adult in all the city who had kept her tongue, and her voice was as refreshing as the throne room's cool, damp air. Before entering, Tutu had been told that he wasn't supposed to look at or stand before the oba, so he just rose to his knees, head bowed, eyes on the sandal straps twisting up the oba's ankles.

"Honored Oba," he said, "this Speaker comes to you as a suckling to the teat. For you are the source of all. The Beginning and End. The Truth and the Lie."

"Eh heh," Oba Ijefi said, satisfied with his supplication. "Continue."

"Honored Oba"—Tutu swallowed—"this Speaker seeks water."

Hushed gasps from the royals.

"So." Tutu couldn't see the oba's face, but he heard the stoniness in her voice. "You think you will succeed where so many have failed, eh?"

"I will succeed," Tutu said. "I know I will succeed."

The gasps became laughter, a round of wet chortles that reminded Tutu of his classmates. They probably thought he was afraid to be cut. That he would rather risk his life on an impossible quest than bear the loss of his tongue. Their mocking made him want to disappear.

But he stayed.

"Speaker," the oba said, voice slow and suspicious. "As you know . . . there are no heroes in the City of Lies."

"No, Honored Oba," he said. "There is one hero in the City of Lies."

The room held its breath, all eyes on Oba Ijefi, waiting. Tutu didn't know the penalty for correcting the oba, but he couldn't save his mama by backing down from anything. He accepted whatever came.

"The Speaker believes himself a hero." Her voice was suddenly warm, and Tutu dared a glance up to see soft eyes and a small, curious smile. "So make him a hero."

At Oba Ijefi's command, Tutu was given a camel—a great big one with intent eyes and a watchful demeanor. He was given an iron spear as long as he was tall, a boiled-hide chest piece with several iron daggers strapped across it, and strips of dried meat and cactus. He was swathed in dark umber cotton to keep the sun from his skin, shod in sturdy but light boots to help protect his feet from scorching sand.

Lastly, he received a canteen of water. He tried to decline it—it was too precious a gift—but an aide to the oba pressed it into his hand. It was more water than he'd ever held before. Enough for at least a week, he thought. Then he saw two more canteens among the packs lashed to his camel.

He almost fainted.

"Thank you, Oba," he said. "But . . ." He couldn't believe he was asking for more after being granted so much. But he wasn't doing any of this for himself. "My mama. She has blood drought. If I am not here to give her water . . ."

Oba Ijefi nodded. "One year, Speaker. The city will water your mama for one year. But after that . . ." She rolled her wrists, palms up, a nonverbal *What more can be done?*

Tutu felt tears coming again, so he quickly fell back to the ground, forehead scraping the floor as he prostrated himself before the oba. *Tears are precious . . .*

He vowed to find water. Not just for his mama, but for the entire city. The oba herself had given him a mission. He couldn't let her down. He couldn't let anyone down.

2

THERE ARE NO FRIENDS *beyond the City of Lies.*

Tutu's first day outside the city walls was spent trudging through the desert. The pockets of sand swirling beneath; the sun burning overhead; the endlessness of the world ahead of him, an infinity for him to explore. In the stories, the Forever Desert was filled with all the worst things the city walls kept out: venomous scavengers, camouflaged predators, massive beasts that could swallow a man whole. And Ajungo, worst of all. Tutu kept alert, fearful of both his apparent solitude and the possibility that he wasn't alone. His camel, who he named Shokolokobangoshe—Bango for short—didn't seem as concerned, often breaking into joyful trots without Tutu's prompting.

Several times, Tutu thought he'd found water. He'd come over a dune and see haze above the sun-soaked sand. But when he urged Bango over, ready to splash into its coolness, he only found the same choked dunes that he'd been riding through for hours. After several of these mirages, he realized that he didn't even know what water was supposed to look like. He knew its feeling well: the cool, rebirthing trickle down the throat. But he'd only ever seen it in a container, the color of an animal skin's dark interior, the smell and taste of boiled, dried meat.

What was a lake? A river? How did an ocean smell? Did water make a sound? If so, did it sound like a jackal braying into the night or like a hot wind blowing down a narrow corridor between homes? These were Tutu's thoughts that first night, laid out on the sleeping mat he'd found among his supplies.

He also thought about his mama. He knew she was worried

about him, but he hoped that the oba's water was helping her recover. He prayed to the gods, asking them to let her know he'd be back soon.

His next three days and nights were the same. The sun raged across the sky, mirage after mirage misled him, and he whispered prayers, scrawling letters to his mama on the parchment of his mind. But he was learning to control Bango better, and he was rationing his water well; he still had two and a quarter skins.

On the fifth day, he found a corpse.

Its skull, spine, and arms poked out of the sand, stripped clean of flesh. The bones were dilapidated, cracked open where some scavengers had gotten at the marrow. Whatever clothes or supplies the person had carried were gone. Who knew how long the man had been dead?

No, not a man.

Not a woman either.

Even if it still wore flesh, the body would've been smaller than his own.

A child.

He buried the bones. Then he said a prayer for the soul of the departed, that it would find water and shade, and that it would be remembered truly. The prayer was a ritual everyone from the City of Lies had memorized, one every child spoke a hundred times before their cutting.

The next day, he found two more corpses. He buried them and prayed for them as well, though he felt uncertainty as he did so.

Where were the corpses coming from?

And why were they all so small?

* * *

His second week was spent traveling through a sandy graveyard. He encountered as many as five corpses a day, in varying states of decay. They were all small, all picked clean of supplies. Many seemed to have died from the heat, with no clear damage to the skeletons beyond the usual decay. But occasionally he came across a body that must have met a violent end—crushed ribs and severed spines, a long crack along the side of a skull.

Beside one of the fresher corpses—one with some remnant of flesh on its bones—he found a pair of parallel gouges in the sand. They were about two body lengths apart and extended to the horizon. He'd seen marks like them before. Every year of his life, he and the other children would climb the towers near the city walls and watch as large wagon wheels cut identical gouges across the desert as they returned to wherever they'd come from, loaded with a fresh harvest of tongues.

The Ajungo.

He made sure to stay far, far away from those wagon tracks.

The final corpse he saw that week snuck up on him. It was buried beneath the sand until Bango stepped on a jut of sharp bone and danced away. Tutu was drinking from his final canteen, and the jolt of movement turned his planned sip into a splash that emptied the rest of the container across his face and onto the sand. Several days of water were lost in an instant.

It was a stupid mistake to make, drinking while in motion. But the days were long, and he was thirsty, and he didn't think anything bad could come from a quick sip. He sucked out the little water that had seeped into his clothes, stoppered the canteen, and closed his eyes.

Tears are precious . . .

All he could imagine was failure. Dying of dehydration out in the desert, leaving his corpse to be found years later by another child playing at hero. The year passing without his return, his mama's supply of water being cut off by the oba. Her terror and confusion from never knowing what had happened to her only remaining child.

He imagined his mama there with him, running her hand

through his hair like she did when he got upset. Eventually that soothed the anger and sorrow and frustration out of him. He rode on.

That night he prayed as he had every night, asking that a message be sent to his mama so that she'd know he was alive. He didn't like to beg the gods—they were busy, he knew—but he added a little prayer for himself, thinking it wouldn't be too selfish given his situation. He prayed for a little water. Not too much, but enough that he could keep going. The whole city needed him, after all.

And the gods answered his prayer.

They said no.

* * *

The next day Tutu tried a new path, turning what he believed to be east. He'd started his journey heading south from the city, and maybe that was the problem. Maybe there was just no water to the south.

For two days, he found only more endless desert, plagued with corpses and mirages and the occasional wagon tracks. Each minute of his trek, he kept his eyes on the horizon, determined not to miss a glimpse of life-saving water. He ate the last of his food, drawing what moisture he could from the chunks of cactus and dried meat. Each night, he prayed desperately, sending thoughts back to his mama, only falling asleep when it took him by force.

On the third day east—the seventeenth of his journey—with his skin thin and mottled from dehydration, his hands shaking on Bango's reins, his eyes perpetually itching no matter how he scratched them, he saw a trio of camel riders on the horizon.

There are no friends beyond the City of Lies.

He was too tired to fight, even if he'd known how. And Bango was too tired to run. So Tutu maintained his usual pace, but angled away from the riders to increase his distance. He wasn't surprised when they stayed parallel with him, watching.

Nor was he surprised when they began to move toward him.

The riders kept the same even pace they'd had all day, an approach so casual that Tutu didn't notice that they'd halved the gap by midday. He turned Bango away at a sharper angle and kicked the poor camel into a trot, thanking her for mustering the strength to flee. By sunset, he could no longer see the three riders in the distance.

That night, he set out his sleep mat and arranged some of his packs on it so that it would look, from afar and in the dark, as if he were laying atop it. Then he moved a short distance away and dug into the bottom slope of a dune until there was enough space for him to slide in and cover himself in sand, leaving only his face unconcealed.

Then he waited.

It wasn't long before two of the riders showed up. They dismounted and walked slow circles around his camp, seemingly watching him sleep. They were both tall and thin, swathed in white silks, with gold jewelry glittering at their wrists and dangling across their foreheads. Strange weapons sat comfortably at their hips: long, coiled whips, each with a three-pronged end that was sharpened and heat-hardened into thick leather claws.

Suddenly, sand trickled down over his face.

He heard a calm and curious voice just above him: "What sort of boy has only a head and sleeps in the sand?"

He tried to draw a dagger and lash out, but he was crushed too tightly by the sand to move. When the voice laughed, he doubled his effort. But he was so tired—so deprived of water and food— that he grew light-headed, and all the world teetered in his vision before closing behind black doors.

3

"BOY? BOY? YA DEAD?"

The first thing Tutu noticed when he woke were the three figures standing over him, shadows against the night sky.

The second thing he noticed was that he wasn't stuck in the dune anymore. He was laid out on his sleep mat beneath the stars, no worse than if he'd set it up himself.

Lastly, he noticed the blessed soft wetness of his throat. The fill in his cheeks. The calm of the itch in his eyes. When you live most of your life without water, you know its feeling like a child knows her mama's scent.

He wasn't thirsty anymore.

"Boy," one of them said, voice thick and flat.

"Maybe he can't speak," said a second, voice delicate and full of concern.

"His throat is broken, this one," the third said, voice high and sarcastic.

"Add more water?"

A canteen appeared, turned over, and poured clear, cool water onto his closed lips, splashing across his face and into his nostrils.

"Stop!" he spluttered, raising his hands to shield his face.

"Boy can speak," said the third voice. "Who knew."

He sat up and blew water out of his nose and onto the sand. Once he regained his breath, he casually looked around for any of his weapons until he found that his daggers were still strapped to his chest.

"Of course Boy can speak," said the second voice. "All boys can speak."

"Unfortunate."

He jumped up and drew iron, hoping to take them by surprise. But when he raised his arm to swing his dagger, one of the attackers touched his shoulder and his arm fell useless at his side, blade slipping from his fingers. He dived forward, tackling one about the waist, but something happened that he didn't understand; he flipped over and over and found himself face first in the sand, a terrible weight on his back.

"Boy, if we wanted ya hurt, ya'd be hurt."

"Ungrateful."

"Get off me!" he screamed.

And they did, just like that.

He scrambled to his feet, rubbing his numbed shoulder.

They stood so calmly they may as well have been frozen. From afar, he'd found them indistinguishable, but by the dim firelight—he'd only just noticed the fire a few paces away, a circle of stones and pile of sticks atop the sand—he could see the differences. The one to the left was a bit shorter and younger than the others, with thick tangles of hair spilling out of the dull white silk wrapped around her head. The one in the center had a nose pushing out of her face like a mountain, and a short chain of gold rings dangled from it. The one to the right might have been the tallest, but stood with a pronounced hunch, as if leaning on an imaginary staff.

They'd pulled him out of the sand, watered him, and let him free when they could've easily kept him pinned. He didn't trust them, but he had to accept that they didn't mean him harm.

There are no friends beyond the City of Lies.

Not yet, at least.

". . . Thank you," he mumbled, and for some reason, that made them laugh. Not like his classmates or how Oba Ijefi's court had laughed, but real, honest laughter. It reminded him of the last time he'd heard real laughter—months back, when he'd put on a puppet show for his mama. Before she'd started spending so much of her days asleep.

"Where ya from, Boy?" the one in the center said, the one with the protruding nose.

She and her companions spoke in a strange melody, like every word had a specific note.

"You . . . you are women," Tutu said, the only thing that came to mind.

Something happened with Nose's hand. Anyone else might have thought it to be a twitch of her fingers, but Tutu was from the City of Lies, where adults couldn't speak.

He knew what a signed language looked like.

"Boy has eyes," said the one on the left, Big Hair. They laughed. Hers was the thick, blunted voice he'd heard before. The same accent as the other two, but different somehow.

"Boy, where ya from?" Nose repeated.

He kept silent. Maybe that was why they hadn't attacked him. Maybe they thought he was one of their own. Or maybe they were afraid—maybe they thought he was Ajungo.

"Again, Boy can't speak," Big Hair said.

"Do ya need more water, little one?" asked the tall one on the right, Hunch, with her delicate voice.

"Where are *you* from?" he shot back.

He'd only said it to slow their questions, but it was even more effective than he imagined. The women fell silent, hesitating, then Nose said, "A town not far. It's small, Boy. Ya wouldn't be like to know the name."

They were Ajungo, Tutu knew. That was why they'd hesitated. That was why they'd lied about being from a "small" place. They weren't sure if he was safe. If he were one of them, they'd be fine. But what if he were from the City of Lies? He could be an advance scout for an invasion. He could have reinforcements on the way.

"I am from a big place," he said. "Many people. And many soldiers too."

They stared at him for a bit, then Nose grinned.

"Well, Boy from a Big Place with Many People and Soldiers," she said, "where ya going?"

"I am looking for water," he admitted. "My canteen is empty."

"We can give you some of—"

"No!" he said. This was what Ajungo did. Give you something simple, then ask an impossible price. Whatever they wanted in exchange for their water, he wasn't willing to pay. No matter how thirsty he was or how cool and delicious their water felt. "I must go," he said, and he began moving past them to where Bango stood.

Thankfully, they parted before him. As he checked his supplies and mounted up, he kept expecting the mood to shift, the attack to come.

But nothing happened.

From atop Bango, he pointed himself toward what he hoped was still east. Almost immediately, one of the women called out to him.

"Boy, if ya need water, ya going the wrong way."

He ignored them. He just needed to round the dune ahead of him and he could gallop off.

"Oasis is the other way!"

He continued a bit farther then stopped. He spoke over his shoulder, frowning. "What is 'oasis'?"

*   *   *

Tutu didn't trust the women. What were they doing wandering the desert? Why did they know how to fight? How had they found water when he hadn't? They were hiding something, he knew, and they weren't as nice as they were making themselves look.

But as he crested the dune to find a lush oasis sitting placidly ahead of them—not a five-minute ride in the opposite direction from where he'd been heading—Tutu didn't care who the women were or what plans they had for him.

He screamed wordless joy as he smacked Bango's rear and urged the camel forward. While jostling atop the charging animal's back, he tore off his boots and pulled his clothes over his head, exposing his sunken torso to the sun. He stood in his saddle, arms out, letting the hot wind howl against his skin. It looked like the sky, the water did. Clear and blue and patient. Like a small disc of sky had fallen asleep and drifted down, down, down to wake surrounded on all sides by burning gold desert and a thin green ring of vegetation.

As Bango slowed near the waterline, Tutu leapt from his mount's back and dived in. He ignored the blunt pain as he slammed into the shallow dirt beneath the water's surface. He ignored the blinding cloud of upset soil floating thick around him. He ignored the sudden plummet of temperature, from molten desert heat to the frigid strangling of every pore.

Water.

Life.

Everything was different under the water. There was a delay when he moved, action disconnected from thought. He marveled at the calm glide of his arms beneath the surface. How the water folded around his fingers as he moved them. The silent drift of the bubbles that escaped his lips. Silent, weightless peace.

Emerging back to the surface was a bittersweet thing.

Tutu spent a long while splashing about and throwing cupped handfuls of water into the air. He took long, blessed gulps until he felt close to bursting. He couldn't stop laughing.

Hours later, when the joy of the experience had become manageable, he refilled his canteens and sat along the edge of the oasis, resting his feet in the water as Bango drank endlessly beside him.

How could there be so much of it? The water was a large circle, three times the length of his body in every direction, bigger than a house. More water than he thought he would see in a dozen lifetimes, just sitting there with no owner, as if no one knew how precious it was.

Only then did he fully realize what he'd accomplished.

He'd saved the City of Lies.

As he watched the cloudy surface of the oasis, he brushed his wrist beneath his weepy nose, wiped tears from his cheeks, and pressed his palms into his eyes. Then he hung his head as the sobs came.

It had been so long since he'd had the freedom to cry. That's what crying was—freedom. You could only cry when there were no more urgent responsibilities. Only when there was no one watching you who depended on your strength. Only when the people around you wouldn't take advantage of your tears.

Only when you had enough water in your body.

Tears are precious . . .

He felt an arm drape over his back, a hip push next to his, and he looked up through shimmery vision to see the tall one, Hunch, holding him protectively, moisture in her own eyes.

He didn't trust her. He didn't trust any of the women. But for a moment, he was back at home, lying beside his mama—her dehydrated bones draped over him, her skin warming his, her scent filling his nose—and he felt wholly and truly safe.

He buried his face in the silks of her clothes and wept himself dry.

4

LATER, THE OTHER WOMEN refilled their canteens and joined him at the water's edge. He asked them all the questions he had in his mind. Where did the water come from? Why didn't it have a sound? Was an oasis the same as an ocean? Why did it look like the sky? Was the sky made of water too? Was rain what happened when the sky fell?

Eventually, Nose held up a hand to stop him. "Boy," she said with equal parts curiosity and confusion, "ya speak like ya don't know water."

Tutu froze. He'd betrayed himself. If he were Ajungo, he would already know all those things.

He had to leave.

"I thank you for your help," he said, springing to his feet. "I must go." He ran over to Bango and climbed into the saddle. He would follow his own tracks until he was home, finding his way by the sun so he could bring his mama and his schoolmates and the oba herself back to the oasis.

"Go where, ya silly boy?" Nose had followed him. She placed a hand on Bango's reins. "Ya can't travel alone."

"I am fine," he said. "Again, I thank you."

"Boy, ya seem new to these lands. Ya don't know the first thing abo—"

She fell silent and looked off across the desert. Tutu turned his gaze to follow hers.

Two round creatures scuttled down a nearby dune. They moved mainly on their hind legs, their front limbs, a pair of little underdeveloped paws, hovering just above the ground. They had dozens of overlapping rings of soft flesh along their backs, and a mound of flesh jutted a half finger out the end of their snouts. As they trailed comfortably past Tutu, he estimated they were nearly as tall as he was, but that they must have been babies by the way they waddled and by their jovial, helpless demeanor.

He stared as they bent down at the oasis and flicked their tongues at the water, taking a nice midday drink.

"Funme!" Nose shouted. "Lami!"

"What?" Hunch shouted back. Then, before Nose could answer, she muttered, "Oh, Goddess blind me." She and Big Hair jumped to their feet and began running to join Nose.

"What is it?" Tutu asked.

"Boy," Nose said. "Move yaself and move yaself quick."

The sand beneath them shivered. Even atop Bango, who stepped uneasily in place, Tutu felt the vibration spear up his spine, setting his teeth a-chatter. Paces ahead of him, the earth erupted. Sand exploded into the air, blinding Tutu and raining cool, dark soil all around him. When it finished falling and he was able to see again, he saw a creature standing across from Nose, regarding her with conflicting impatience and curiosity. It was a replica of the two babies that had waddled past them earlier, only ten times the size. The ringed flesh on its back was a hard armor; the fleshy mound on the end of its snout a curved and pointed horn that was as long as a man was tall.

Nose faced the creature unafraid, legs bent sturdy against the ground, clawed whip in her hand. Hunch ran off to the side of the beast, whooping and shouting to get its attention, while Big Hair kept her distance, irritably tying her mass of curls back from her eyes.

The beast dipped its head and horn in Nose's direction, a false charge meant to intimidate. But Nose stood her ground. It tossed its head a second time, bringing the tip of its horn closer, but again Nose didn't move.

The third time was meant to kill.

The beast's thick neck jerked up, its horn ripping through the air where Nose had stood the moment before. But she'd dived away, rolled back up to her feet, and cracked her whip. The long coil unfurled across the sky and snapped at the beast's head, wrapping around its horn.

With an angry snort, the beast reared back, yanking the whip from Nose's grasp so forcefully Tutu could almost feel the skin of her palm burn away.

From another angle, Hunch launched her own attack, whip lashing out once, twice, three times, scraping skin from the monster's heel and drawing its attention. It forgot about Nose, turning to Hunch and charging horn first.

Hunch rolled away, surprisingly agile for a woman so big, and ran over to join Nose.

"Boy!" Nose shouted. "Move yaself, ya stupid boy!"

By the time Tutu realized he was in the beast's sights, that he hadn't moved at all the first time Nose told him to, it was too late.

He'd always considered himself brave. He never backed down when his classmates made fun of him, which they did often. He'd fought bigger boys, knowing he'd lose, and gone home with his face held high despite the lumps and bruises he wore. But as he looked directly at the tip of death's mindless charge, his terror was so complete he couldn't even scream. How quickly his success had turned to failure, water to dust. He'd failed to complete the quest he set for himself. He'd failed the city and all the people who depended on his finding water.

He'd failed his mama, who had battled death half a hundred times so that he wouldn't have to.

There are no heroes in the City of Lies.

The sun shone off the point of the beast's horn, half a breath from driving up through Bango and Tutu both.

Then Big Hair slid into view, her skin sparkling so faintly that

Tutu wasn't sure what he was seeing. As the massive beast bore down on her, she reared back, then brought her head forward, bashing her tiny skull into the tip of the animal's massive horn. Tutu didn't want to watch the woman die, but he couldn't look away.

Stunningly, her head didn't burst. Instead, she smashed the horn to pieces, length by length exploding outward as her head drove down, until her forehead met the beast's and the air filled with a concussive clap.

The beast dropped, silent as stone.

Big Hair's sparkle dissipated. She shared brief looks and warm hand holds with the other women, each ensuring the others were unharmed.

Then Nose turned to him. "Are ya fine, Boy?"

He didn't know what to say. He bent forward on Bango, eyes wide, wrapping his arms around his stomach as he reeled from the emotional whiplash of the day.

He felt a hand close on his shoulder and he instinctively pulled back, tugging Bango a couple steps away. He took a long look at the women. They weren't his mama. No one was his mama. But they had led him to water, consoled him, saved his life.

There are no friends beyond the City of Lies.

"I am fine," he said. And he meant it. "I am fine."

* * *

They convinced him to stay in the area for a while, insisting that he was too shaken up to travel. Together, they set up camp a safe distance away from the oasis, close enough to easily refill their canteens but far enough away to avoid any other thirsty beasts. Starlight beamed down from the clear desert sky above as they settled in for the night.

They talked. Tutu learned their names—Nose, Hunch, and Big Hair became Asilah, Funme, and Lami—and that, though their faces bore the resemblance of sisters, they were cousins, traveling together for safety.

"Why do you travel?" Tutu asked.

The cousins shared a glance, then Asilah's eyes looked to Tutu's spear propped against the side of the tent.

"We are searching, Boy," she said. "For iron."

"You cannot find iron?" In the City of Lies, iron was almost as common as sand.

She shook her head, her nose rings jingling. "We got none where we from."

"Where is that?" Tutu asked.

They shared a look again. This time, Hunch—Funme—spoke in that delicate voice of hers.

"Long ago, little one, before ya baba and mama made ya, we lived in a great land. We could eat, drink, and sleep and know our young ones were safe. Because our Goddess was always watching."

Funme nodded at Big Hair, Lami, who turned her wrist this way and that, showing off the smooth, black stones of the bracelet she wore. Black was a rare color in the desert. In the stories, it was always the color of power.

"What are those?" Tutu asked.

"God's Eyes," Asilah said. "Some of us"—she nodded at Lami, who shrugged—"are blessed to use Her eyes for protection. We call them Seers."

"One in a million," Lami said, cracking open a peanut shell and tossing a nut into her mouth.

Tutu remembered Lami tying up her hair before the beast attacked. She'd used the bracelet—the God's Eyes—as a hair band.

"Our Goddess don't much like iron," Funme continued. "It's the one thing she can't See. So when our iron mines collapsed, what did it matter to us? We had clay for pots, stone and wood for building. We needed no spears—Her Eyes, and Seers like Lami, kept us safe. Instead of mining iron all day or training to fight, our men learned to sing. They were the sweetest singers in the Forever Desert."

"But our enemies were watching," Asilah said. "They came one day like a storm, with iron of their own. They cut down our Seers. They murdered our men, and any boy who looked the part. They destroyed our city. Then they disappeared, like an owl in the sun."

Lami sucked her teeth in disgust.

"We were helpless," Funme said, picking up the story. "And with no Seers came the Silence, with all the devilish creatures of the dark roaming our city year after year after year as we huddled in the dark. Children grew old without ever leaving their homes. But after many long years of suffering, our enemies returned with an offer. They would give us iron."

"For what?" Tutu asked.

Asilah looked at him for a long moment before speaking. "Ears," she said. "The ears of every woman in our city, and her hearing with it. When a girl becomes a woman, they cut her ears and burn closed the hole. We could have our iron. We could have our training and swords. But what good is an army that cannot hear orders?"

"Even worse," Funme added, seemingly hunching more as the story went on, "what good are the sweetest singers in the Forever Desert when none have ears to hear them?"

Unbidden, the image of his mama with severed ears came to Tutu's mind. He swallowed, throat full of sick.

"But you all have your ears," he said. "Did you escape?"

It happened again. Asilah's fingers flashed, and this time Tutu caught some of the words.

. . . you have ears . . . run away.

The signs weren't the same as those used in his city, but they were close enough that he was confident—Asilah was repeating what he'd just said.

"Many of us do," Asilah said, "Every year. We leave in groups, often with sisters or cousins. Myself and Funme left as girls. We've lived in this cursed desert, trying to survive."

"So much we left behind," Funme added with a distant look.

Asilah spared a kind glance for her cousin. "We did."

Tutu looked at Lami. "And what about you?"

Asilah's fingers echoed him.

"Many of us escape, little one," Funme said sadly. "But not all of us."

Lami pushed back the hair along the sides of her head, revealing two scorched mangles of flesh, the cauterized remains of her ears.

"The only time we've returned home was for Lami's deafening," Asilah said. "We tried to free her, but we were too late."

Lami shrugged and let her hair fall back into place.

"So . . . she is . . . ?" He didn't know the word for someone who couldn't hear.

"Deaf," Asilah offered. "But she's a Seer. She had good eyes."

Only then did Tutu realize that Lami, as relaxed and aloof as she seemed, kept careful watch of her cousins as they spoke, tracking the movements of their mouths. Asilah only seemed to translate when Tutu spoke, the movements of his mouth unfamiliar to Lami.

He thought over their story, putting the pieces together into a familiar tale to which he already knew the ending. "That is why you do not have spears. Your enemy gave you iron, but it was not enough. Or it was enough but not good."

Asilah snorted. "Iron not fit to boil water in, much less fight with. You know our enemy, Boy?"

He looked from one woman to the other, unsure of what he was about to say. Could he trust them? Did he have a choice?

There are no friends beyond the City of Lies.

It was hard to overrule years and years of honed mistrust.

"What is the name of your enemy?" he asked.

Asilah signed his words and the women shared a look. It was Lami who broke the stare, seemingly irritated.

"He is a boy. A thin boy." She turned her attention to Tutu. "Our enemy is the Ajungo."

He must have reacted, because all three women frowned.

"You know them?" Asilah asked.

*   *   *

He told them everything.

It was so freeing to share the secrets he'd stowed away in his heart. These women weren't Ajungo. They were his saviors, and his friends, and they hated the Ajungo as much as he did.

He told them all the stories his mama and his teachers had told him, passed down from the Greatmamas before them. He told them about the Fever and the exchange made and the cutting and how the Ajungo went back on their deal. He told them of his mama's blood drought and his mission to bring back water even though everyone had ridiculed him. Even though so many had tried and failed.

"But I did it," he said, suddenly exhausted. "I have enough water for everyone."

Asilah tilted her head, confused. "How many are in ya city, Boy?" He'd told them his name was Tutu, but that didn't seem to matter to them.

"Thousands," he said shrugging. "I do not know. Many thousands."

"Little one . . ." Funme said, her voice soft. "With rain, that oasis can only water a hundred. Maybe two hundred. To water a city, ya need a river."

He stared, waiting for them to laugh at the joke. But they didn't.

"All that water?" he said. "It must be for a city."

Funme shook her head. "An oasis is not for so many," she said.

"Ya drink a little and maybe more comes later. But ya can't drink every day. Day and day and day, a hundred people? Drinking and washing and watering camels? In a week, ya going to have just sand and nothing else."

"Oh," he said. He took a long, long breath, thinking of his mama. Of course it wasn't that easy. He should have known. All those who had left the city and never returned. If it were as simple as finding an oasis—and it sounded like there was more than just the one—the city would have been saved long ago.

He suggested a trade—their city's water in exchange for his city's iron. But even their city lacked a river. It had a lake that collected mountain runoff during the rare rains. They had plenty of water in the good times, but one missed storm and that could change. The only thing they were confident their oba would trade were the God's Eyes. They had plenty.

Unfortunately, God's Eyes would not slake the thirst of Tutu's people.

He had one year, though. It had only been a few weeks, and look how much he had found. He had a year. He would find a river. More than that; he would find an ocean, which he had learned was even bigger than a river.

"Did they change your name too?" he asked.

The women looked confused.

"The Ajungo," he said. "They changed the name of our city. Now we have a bad name."

Asilah translated for Lami—who snorted and looked away— before responding. "They said they took our ears because we were mad and heard evil whispers," she said. "They said they gave us poor iron because we were violent. Savages. And after the bastards had served up this nonsense to all who could hear, they named us so that none would ever believe if we told them otherwise."

"The City of Lies," Tutu said.

Surprise, then understanding, dawned on their faces.

It was the one thing he hadn't told them. He'd feared it would poison everything he'd said prior, to admit to being from a land of liars. But now he understood why the Ajungo cut out the tongues of his people. He understood what it meant that he was a Speaker.

The women shared a look, then Asilah nodded. "Different cities, same name," she said. Then her eyes narrowed. "Same enemy."

5

FROM THEN ON, they traveled together. They switched to evening travel—riding in the heat of the day was foolish, the cousins explained. They searched the desert for water, letting the moonlight guide them, following any glint they saw on the horizon. They never found a river, sometimes found an oasis. Mostly, though, they found empty expanses of gold-red sand.

Cautious to preserve what they could until they found another meal, they ate what the land offered. Occasionally, they'd come across a copse of cacti or pluck withered berries from parched bushes. Sometimes they'd even find a nest and enjoy a meal of eggs, then Funme would set a trap for the mother and not long after they'd be plucking, gutting, and salting vulture meat.

Just before dawn, the coolest part of each day, Asilah taught Tutu to fight. She didn't know the spear, but she taught him to fight with stick and whip, showed him how to make and aim a sling, and helped him train his body for the graceful dance of unarmed violence. The first weeks were exhausting and boring, full of repetitive movements that he had to perform until his muscles gave out on him. Eventually, though, his body hardened, and the repetition wasn't so tiring. After that, Asilah began to teach him all sorts of new ways to destroy the human body.

He picked it up quickly. Not because he had any special talent, but because he didn't have much else to think about all day except fighting. Before long he began training alongside the women, trading strikes and holds, whip against whip. As the months passed, his body grew as much as his fighting skills. He gained half a hand in height and every part of him thickened noticeably, enough that

Funme had to protect him from Asilah and Lami's merciless taunts about how handsome he was becoming.

The training, as difficult as it was, proved far easier than the search. Even though Asilah was a skilled navigator, they were frequently lost, certain that the cliffs to the east were the same cliffs they'd seen to the west a month before, or certain that they'd circled back to the same dunes from a week prior. Sandstorms would block them from travel, and giant, wild beasts would force them off course, often delaying their access to water when they needed it.

Every night, he thought about his mama. She must have long since recovered from her blood drought. He wondered what her life was like without him. Had she gone back to work, braiding hemp ropes for the well-search teams? Did she still wear her wide-brimmed hat over her hair cover to help keep the sun off her skin? Did she still say good night to the lizard in the corner of their house, who had become their pet out of circumstance and earned his keep by eating spiders? He wondered if she would even recognize him now. She had always worried he would be short forever—*eat your gari so you do not have to live a short man's life*—but now he was almost as tall as she was, maybe even taller. He wondered, with how big he was, if she would still let him sleep with his head in her lap.

The longer he was away from his mama, and the more days that passed without finding any water, the more he began to lose hope that he would ever see her again.

"Husband!" Asilah called. It was the first day of the sixth month since he'd left home. They'd set up camp in the shade of a tall dune, just as the sun was waking. "Come and tell us a story."

Tutu finished tying up the camels and made his way back to the campfire. "Why me?" he asked.

"Because ya wives are tired," she said. "And unhappy. Come be a man with big muscles and good stories."

He sat next to Funme, suppressing the urge to rest his head on her shoulder—it was a habit he was trying to break. Across the fire, Asilah sat cross-legged and Lami lay on her sleeping mat, head propped up in her palm.

"When I was a boy," he began, ignoring Lami's snort, "I heard the story of Obasa's Shadow. You know it?" When they all shook their heads, he continued. "Obasa was oba of a big southern land, and he had many riches. But one day, he found his favorite ring was gone. It was a ring passed down from his greatbaba and his greatbaba's greatbaba. He called all his court together. 'We have a thief in the palace!' he said. 'Anyone who finds this thief will be given ten goats and one hundred chickens.'"

"One hundred chickens!?" Asilah sucked her teeth. "A man will give ya work and name it a gift." Lami barked a laugh.

"Continue, my Tutu," Funme said, shooting a look at her cousins.

"No one went to Obasa about the thief, until one day Obasa woke and his favored son was gone. So Obasa again gathered his court. 'We have a kidnapper in the palace. Anyone who finds this kidnapper will be given two hundred acres of land and fifty cows.'"

"Fifty!?" Asilah exclaimed. She sucked her teeth again. "This Obasa is a wicked man." Even Funme laughed at that, but she rubbed Tutu's back gently, urging him on.

"Again, no one went to Obasa. Years passed, and one day Obasa woke up in an empty field, as far as the eye could see. He looked around, but he could find not one piece of his palace or any of his possessions. Around him, all the people of his land were standing in the same field. All of them looked confused. Obasa said, 'A devil has taken my kingdom while I slept! Anyone who finds this devil will be made my counselor and will live in comfort with children and grandchildren for all the days my family rules this land.' Finally, someone stepped forward, a simple old man who had tended the palace's guava before they disappeared. He said he knew who the thief, kidnapper, and devil were, and they were one and the same."

"Good," Asilah said, "tell us the end to this story, old man with no guavas."

But Tutu was staring off at the horizon, where a plume of sand-smoke curled up into the air, dark against the marooning sunrise. The sort of plume that came from a galloping beast.

"Old men don't need guavas anyhow," Lami said with a small smile.

Asilah cackled. "Blind old man. If he could not find his guavas, why did he not ask his wife?"

"Two bad-mouthed women," Funme said, stifling laughter. "Finish ya story, my Tutu. Tutu?"

Not a galloping beast. The plume was too large. Beasts. It grew closer, larger, revealed itself to be led by a line of black dots. The women looked back over their shoulders, following his gaze. Asilah stood and shielded her eyes from the sun. "Blessed Eyes . . . are those camels?"

As far as Tutu could tell, they were. Camels at full speed.

"People?" Funme asked. "Ajungo?"

Tutu's blood froze. Who else would roam the desert so brazenly? Who else had five—no, ten; they were in two rows—camel riders to spare on a mission in the desert waste?

"We must hide," he hissed. "We must hide!"

But they all knew it was too late for hiding. They'd set up their camp. They could either flee, leaving all their supplies behind, or they could confront the riders. Asilah grabbed her whip and went over to untie the camels. Lami rose calmly to her feet, peering across the sand. Funme was suddenly standing behind him with a hand on his shoulder.

"Be ready, my Tutu. And don't speak."

Once Asilah brought over the camels, they all mounted up,

and by then the riders were within shouting distance. Tutu saw they were all in red silk, with thick leather armor strapped to their chests, and . . .

"Iron," he muttered.

Solid iron spears, longer than he was tall, bounced in the men's hands as they trotted toward Tutu and the women. Asilah nodded to Funme and the two walked their mounts forward, leaving Tutu and Lami a few lengths behind.

The Ajungo had stolen iron from the women's land. They would have plenty for such weapons. But Tutu recognized the red silk. He'd seen it before, in the Palace of Lies, wrapping the oba and all her court.

These men weren't Ajungo.

They were from home.

One man, with a gold vulture crest set in the center of his head wrap, heeled his mount ahead of the others. "We have no quarrel with you women," he said. "We just want to see this young man."

Tutu stared, confused. He could talk. He had a tongue.

"And who is 'we'?" Asilah asked.

"We are envoys from Oba Ijefi."

The sweet pain of hope panged in his heart, a longing he hadn't known he possessed.

For a moment, the confusion in his mind warred with the longing in his heart, half of him mistrustful, and half of him willing to trust anything. But soon, all parts of him came into alignment. Their leader, the man with the tongue, was like him. A Speaker. He must have escaped his own cutting and spent years roaming the desert. All these men could be the Tutus of the past, the few who had escaped the fate of the desert's skeletons.

"I am Tutu!" he shouted, ignoring Lami's grip on his forearm. He shrugged her off and urged Bango forward past Asilah and Funme. "I am Tutu! I left six moons ago to find water."

And he'd failed. Maybe that's why the men had found him. Maybe they were there to help.

"Is my mama alive?" Tutu asked, and once he said it, he felt a shift inside him from hope to despair. As he waited for the answer, all he could hear was his own loud, constricted breathing, and all he could feel was the rapid march of his heart. He'd asked the question before thinking whether he could bear the answer. "She promised," he croaked out, tears building in his eyes. He didn't even blink them back; he was too scared to be ashamed. "Oba Ijefi promised one year of water. One year!"

The cousins were looking at him, but he couldn't tell what their faces—blurry and wet on the edge of his vision—were saying. Lami moved closer to him on her camel, and he felt her hand on his back. She'd never been gentle with him like that before. Her hand was the only thing that kept him from sliding out of his saddle.

The man tilted his head. "Your mama is well," he said as if it were the simplest thing, as if wellness were guaranteed.

It took Tutu several moments to believe the words, to trust that their truth wouldn't evaporate.

"Fine . . ." He blinked away the tears, looked up and down the row of men. "So why have you come?"

"We have found water," he said. "We are here to bring you home."

Home.

In that moment, the last half year seemed so senseless. Wandering the desert, scarcely surviving dehydration, evading monsters and the elements and starvation and despair. And he'd done most of it as a boy, a child who didn't even know what he was looking for, who'd thought a pond in the desert could slake a city's thirst.

"The boy is home with us," Asilah said.

Tutu stared at her, certain he'd misheard.

"Go on now," Funme added. "He does not need ya. Go on back to your City of Lies." She spat the last part.

The women must have been blinded by the name of the city, Tutu thought, just like the Ajungo had hoped. They didn't trust these men from his home. They didn't believe that anyone from the City of Lies could bear the truth.

"This is our second warning," the man said, his tone as sharp as his spearpoint. "And our last. Give the boy over."

"I will go!" Tutu shouted. He whipped Bango into motion, but as he passed Asilah and Funme, the latter snatched his reins and yanked his mount to a halt.

"Tutu! Stay, my Tutu."

He tried to jerk his arm away once, twice, but her grip was iron. She was trying to keep him from his mama, he realized. They all were. They wanted him to roam the desert with them forever, hungry and thirsty and lost. Because their city had failed to get what it needed. They had no home to return to.

But he did.

"Let go of me," he said, anger bubbling, staring up into Funme's dark, concerned eyes. "I am not yours! You are not my mama!"

She let him go immediately and with a sharp intake of breath, as if his words were a whip that had bitten hot into her flesh. Her face shimmered like desert heat, a wavering mirage that could've been either shame or heartbreak.

Tutu turned away from her, rode past Asilah's outstretched hand, and over to the men. He turned to face the women who had cared for him the last half year and saw Asilah suppressing rage, Lami quiet and alert, Funme in broken disbelief, posture saggy in her saddle.

"I am sorry," he said, and he meant it. He didn't wish them harm, but sometimes a man had to make difficult decisions, and he'd made his. The women had a hard desert life ahead, and he wanted the best for them. But he wouldn't be joining them.

"Boy, come back," Asilah said. "Ya don't understand."

"I am sorry."

Lami finally spoke in her thick voice. For some reason, she was tying her hair up in her band of God's Eyes, readying for battle. "The desert is full of dead boys like yaself, and ya think these lizards are here to save ya? A damn fool." Her skin began to sparkle in the way it had before, like every bit of skin reflected a slightly different light.

There are no friends beyond the City of Lies.

Tutu looked at the man with the golden vulture crest. Really looked at him, and his men. Maybe their spears were to protect Tutu for the trip home. Or to fight off beasts and Ajungo. Maybe the vulture didn't mean what the sight of vultures always meant—a fresh kill, leftovers to scavenge. Maybe it was just for decoration.

Maybe. But he couldn't ignore the fact that no child who went looking for water had ever returned.

Asilah struck first.

6

ASILAH'S WHIP CRACKED, followed by an alarmed squeal from the Vulture's camel. A three-forked tongue of skin disappeared from the man's hand, and he dropped his iron spear. He glanced down at the blood, sighed, then looked up at the women.

"Kill them," he said. "The boy first."

Her whip cracked again, this time right by Tutu's head. He felt a spearpoint dig fire across his temple as he urged Bango back toward the women, ignoring the hot stream of blood dribbling down his head and neck.

Asilah and Funme charged forward to cover his retreat, lashing out with their whips. But the men were numerous and well-trained, and in seconds they'd formed a circle around Tutu and the cousins, spears leveled.

Lami, skin sparkling, spanked her mount forward as well, heading right for the center spearman who was protecting the Vulture. First, she backhanded the point of the soldier's spear. It ripped from his grip as if he were a child and drove into the man beside him so forcefully the man was lifted from his saddle and into the sky before being pinned into the sand ten strides away. She then brought her other hand down on his camel's head, snapping its neck, a grotesque sound of pain issuing from its mouth. The soldier pitched forward on the destroyed animal, and Lami caught him by his throat. She raised him in the air, then turned just in time to use him as a shield as a spear punched into his torso.

As Lami singlehandedly collapsed the attackers' center, Asilah and Funme whipped at the right flank. Tutu unholstered his whip and joined them, snapping a blow at the nearest enemy.

The soldier raised his spear, let Tutu's whip wrap around its head, then tugged. Tutu should have let go—he wasn't strong enough to win a pulling match—but instead he held on and was torn from his saddle, landing hard and headfirst.

He climbed to his knees, eyes blinded by sand. Spears hissed by him; sharp-toed camel feet kicked; whips cracked; fists and bodies hurtled about, landing with sick, wet thuds. He pawed at his face with one hand while scrambling for his whip with the other, the blood and thunder of battle raging around him.

"Tutu!" He heard Funme's voice, felt her gentle hand on his shoulder. "Stay, I have you."

When he cleared his eyes, he saw that the battle had changed much in so short a time.

Of the ten riders, four were dead—the two Lami had killed to start the melee and two others, one still with a hand around his throat, failing to stem the red-black leakage of life through his fingers. Asilah had been thrown from her camel and sported a gash along her cheek, bad enough that another hair deeper would've earned her a second mouth. Her whip was cut in half, a useless length of leather. Funme was also on foot, weary but uninjured other than a row of cracked, bloody knuckles on her whip hand that said she must have struck something. Two of the surviving men stood across from Asilah and Funme. The other four, including the Vulture, had Lami trapped at the center of their square formation, each of their spears leveled at her head.

Lami moved first, spitting at one man while charging another. She dove off her mount and rolled horizontally through the air while her spit took its target in his eye—he released a haggard scream that said he knew he would never use the eye again. She tumbled through the spindly front legs of the enemy soldier's camel to the sound of a grotesque and disquieting pair of fleshy snaps.

As Lami fought, spears stabbed down at Asilah and Funme like the stingers of giant bees. The cousins counterattacked, Funme with her whip and Asilah with a handful of sand. But they were woefully outmatched. On the soldiers' charge, Asilah dodged a spearpoint only to receive a camel's kick square in her gut. Funme avoided any fatal blows but was cut by each of her enemy's three rapid thrusts.

Both women were too busy fighting for their lives to save Lami.

Two riders set upon the Seer just as she got back to her feet. When the first man stabbed down, Lami punched up at the spearpoint. Were it anything else in the world, her fist would have destroyed it, burst through it like an axe through rotted wood.

But the spearhead was iron, the one thing her Goddess couldn't See. The point slid into her knuckles, exploded through the bones of her wrist, drove deep into her forearm.

Lami didn't scream. She just stared in confusion at her blasted limb and then, as she seemed to realize what had happened, drooped her face into an expression of relaxation, even boredom.

The Vulture, with his golden emblem flashing in the sunlight, drove his spear through her back, her spine, her heart.

Tutu was already running toward her. The remaining boy in him, naive to the world, thought he would play the hero by swooping in to save her. The unlikely apprentice rescuing the wounded master.

He caught her around the neck just as she collapsed into the sand. He'd never seen so much blood. An endless pool, as if an oasis of blood were forming before him. He'd seen plenty of death, but death by heat was a bloodless thing. Slow and silent. This death was so sudden, so loud, so terrible.

As he stared into her eyes, unable to do anything but stare, he caught the scent of her hair. It smelled like the desert: parched and unpredictable. But with a single, defiant fragrance of wild-flower. He knew she put on perfume every day before they set out on their ride, no matter how senseless it seemed. But he'd never actually smelled it before.

Her eyes rolled in her head before settling on Tutu.

Then the sparkle of her skin faded. Lami was gone.

Tutu, oblivious to the Vulture drawing another spear, moved a hand to touch her dimming God's Eyes. When his palm—a man's palm, roughened by desert life and the grip of his training whip—ran along the black stones, the world went white.

In the quiet and endless expanse of whiteness, he saw his mama, whose face was full again, alive with water, hair thick and fine like she was a young girl. She smiled, and he realized that she looked like him. Or he looked like her. They were one and the same, a spirit split only by time and distance.

Then she was gone, replaced by the chaotic and blood-soaked desert. Except everything was clearer than before. Tutu couldn't just see the sand and the soldiers and the mayhem. He could see the sun rolling crimson up the horizon. See Asilah and Funme behind him, still unaware that their cousin was dead. See a family of desert rodents burrowing into a patch of shaded sand. See the far away pungent scent of a sun-bloated carcass, a wild cat that had failed too many hunts and succumbed to the heat. See the taste of Asilah's tears, the throbbing of her screaming throat as she realized that she'd lost one of the people she loved most in the world.

Tutu saw the Vulture hop down from his camel and raise his spear in both hands like he was preparing to plant a flag. Tutu saw the man's fear. He saw his bravery too. He saw his sense of humor and his love of raising rabbits and his violent temper and how tired he was in the mornings and how restless he was at night. Saw his confusion over the order to kill another child in the desert. Saw his regret at killing innocent women, even ones who had attacked him. Saw his justifications for all those atrocities, his acceptance of the lies he'd been told and the lies he'd told himself. Lies and lies and lies stacked one atop another.

A one-man city of lies.

Before the Vulture brought his spear down, Tutu met him with a slap to the body, a move Asilah had taught him. When his palm connected with the man's torso, his body simply moved. A large chunk of it shifted off in several directions, exposing him down to the spine, his innards a drifting cloud of fleshy debris.

Tutu felt the slap as well, in the same spot he'd hit the man. Unlike his foe, Tutu's body remained intact, but the pain was every bit as violent. His entire body seized up and went numb, and he was thrown on the sand, unable to move, unable to think.

He'd slain their golden vulture, though. Their commander. The fount of their lies. Without leadership, surrounded by the wreckage of life around them, the remaining men wheeled their camels and fled.

Tutu shivered in the sand. He tried and failed to breathe as his body rebelled against him. Funme slid over beside him, blood splashed on her face. Her whip hand was missing, hacked away in jagged cuts as if amputated by an amateur. She held him delicately in her one good hand, and her eyes were scared only for him, as if she had nothing to fear for herself. For a moment, as his body was wracked by seizure and his grasp on consciousness loosened, he thought she was his mama, holding him through a fever, ignoring her own health for his.

7

DREAMS ARE PREPARATION.

That was what his mama had taught him. From a young age, the first thing he'd done each morning, even before dry-washing his face for school, was tell his mama his dream from the night before. Good or bad, he would recount them, and she would take them as seriously as if they were real events.

There are no lions here, she signed one summer, back when he was a boy, *but one day a lion will chase you again, and because of that dream you will be ready.*

She made him study his dreams all morning, recalling the details as he brushed his teeth, imagining other ways the dream could have gone as he changed into his school clothes, practicing those better ways over and over as he strolled with his friends to the schoolhouse. When he returned home, he'd report back to her.

"I will throw sand in the lion's eye," he said that night.

Eh heh. Why not hide?

"Lions can smell very good."

Why not climb to a roof?

"What if there is no roof?"

Good. And why not call for your mama? she asked, pulling him into her lap, burying her nose in his hair.

"Because mama does not like lions either."

My smart son! She smiled.

* * *

Tutu woke to a dark sky. Moonless, with stars like distant and dimming torches, failing to illuminate the desert.

His body had healed. But for a general ache in his bones, he didn't feel any lingering injuries from the battle. He took a deep breath and sat up to find Asilah standing across from a strange man.

He scrambled for his whip, his knives, anything he could use to kill the man where he stood, but Funme put her remaining hand on his shoulder, soothing him.

"Ya safe now, my Tutu. Ya safe."

There are no friends beyond the City of Lies.

"Who is he?" Tutu asked.

This man did not wear red silks nor bear a golden vulture. He was lighter-skinned than the other men, golden as the sun and hairless except for a thin, braided beard. He didn't have the soldiers' beguiling look, their subtle masquerade of humanity— rather, he looked disciplined, stern, as dry and drawn as the desert itself.

But Tutu knew now that the desert was a killing ground. Even men from his own home sought to harm him. This stranger couldn't be trusted.

"Who are you?" Tutu called, ignoring Funme's hush.

Asilah and the man glanced at him. Or, rather, Asilah did. The man turned his head in Tutu's direction, but his eyes were shut. Not clasped together shut, but sewn shut; loops of thread stitched top eyelid and bottom into one.

"Young Tutu," the man said. His voice was dry and bumpy, like a stick dragging over hollow stone. He had a different accent from Asilah and Funme. It moved from high to low by the end of the phrase like a whistle, and he extended the *ooo*'s in Tutu's name. "I have heard your story, young Tutu. You have many things in this desert you need fear, eh? The sun and thirst. The snakes and jackals. The lying waters and boastful sands. You need fear the will of the gods—they have already taken one of your mothers, I am told."

Tutu wanted to say that Lami was not his mama, that he had a mama and a home, but he remembered that Lami was dead. In life, she was often very distant. But sometimes, when he was doing some late evening chore, she would watch for a while, then say something like, "Your mama is a good woman. Very good woman." And it would both fill him with confusion and make him hold his chest high.

She wouldn't say those nice things to him anymore.

So instead of telling the man that Lami wasn't his mama, he didn't say anything.

"You need fear many men, young Tutu, but not I," the man finished, and he dipped in a slight bow.

Tutu wasn't convinced. "Why are you here?" he asked.

"Same as you! Same as your mothers and their mothers before them. Because this is my story."

The man was strong. Tutu could see that now, just from a glance. He was half a hand shorter than Funme but denser, with wide, stable shoulders. He was a warrior.

"What happened to your eyes?" Tutu asked.

"Tutu!" Funme scolded.

The man approached slowly, each foot feeling out the sand for just a moment before settling to let the next foot search its own way forward. When he was a stride away, he sat, legs crossed, the skin of his eyes directed at Tutu.

"I am from a city far from here, young Tutu. A city that sits on the banks of three rivers."

Three rivers. Tutu felt his spirit tremble as the words sank into him. Three.

Three rivers.

"We lived mostly on the water. When we were not fishing, we were swimming. When we were not swimming, we were bathing. Each night before we sank into sleep, we all looked down into one of the three rivers and bid a long rest to our ancestors. And our ancestors looked back up at us. Boys saw their fathers. Mothers saw their daughters. All who perish are taken into the water, where they remain to counsel future generations and smile upon our successes."

"But . . ." Tutu said. He already knew where the story would turn. It seemed to be the only story there was.

"But," the man said, head tilting up to the night sky as if he could still see it, "the Ajungo came."

When one of their rivers flooded, they were able to manage. When the second flooded, it took everything they had to keep the waters from rushing through their city.

Then the third river flooded and the Ajungo appeared.

They offered a supernatural solution—special stones called God's Eyes that would give the drowning citizens great power. They could force the rivers back within their banks. They could reshape the land to chart new courses for the water. They could even ask their ancestors what offense had been committed to deserve such flooding.

But the God's Eyes would come at a price.

"Eyes for eyes," Tutu said.

"Indeed."

"And you accepted."

"How could we not?"

They shared a long silence.

"What else?" Tutu asked.

The Blind Man tilted his head. It was difficult to understand his eyeless expressions, but Tutu felt his confusion.

"You did not come into the desert for your eyes," Tutu said. "You must need something. Something the Ajungo did not give."

The Blind Man smiled. "How old are you, young Tutu?"

"Thirteen." His birthday had been so long ago. He'd never even celebrated.

"Then you are a clever boy of thirteen," the Blind Man responded. "The Ajungo would not give us God's Eyes. They would only lend us Seers. Their Seers came and calmed our rivers, then disappeared back into the Forever Desert. Yet every year since, all three rivers have flooded. And each time, we must trade eyes for eyes."

Just then, everything Tutu had learned over the last six months came together with chilling clarity.

"You have water, but need Eyes," he said to the Blind Man. Then he looked at Asilah. "You have Eyes, but need iron. And I . . ." He looked down at the sand, ashamed of how young and foolish he'd been. ". . . I have iron, but need water."

"And yet all of us," the Blind Man said, "are from the same place."

"The City of Lies," Asilah said.

The Ajungo had done it to three different cities: preyed on the people's desperation, offered them a broken deal, then named them liars. But how? How much power did the Ajungo have? What else were they capable of?

"This is not a problem for ya head, my Tutu," Funme said.

"He is no longer a boy, Funme," Asilah countered.

Tutu didn't understand. "What problem?" he asked.

"I am not here in search of Eyes, clever Tutu," the Blind Man said. "Eyes for my people only means more Eyes for the Ajungo, for they will surely take whatever they must to keep control. No, I am here in search of help. This is no life we live, roaming the desert in hopes of tripping over water or iron or eyes of gods. I want to end it all. To break the cycle. To find the true source of our troubles."

The Ajungo.

Tutu watched the Blind Man with suspicion. He was only in the desert to find water. That was why he'd left his city, left his mama, risked death for months. Endured all the mirages and oasis beasts and moments of deep despair. Spent all those nights praying his mama could forgive him for another night away.

There is no water in the City of Lies.

Then he finally found a man from a land with three rivers, and this man wanted him to forget about water? To instead face an enemy powerful enough to control three cities? To confront the Ajungo themselves?

"This is not ya fight," Funme said to him softly. "Get ya water and go home, my Tutu."

"Will you help him?" Tutu asked.

She looked back with soft, apologetic eyes. "I must."

He looked to Asilah, and she nodded. "Ya still young, Tutu. When ya reach our age, understanding comes—evil in one place is evil in every place. We will help this man."

Tutu chewed his lip, thinking. What if this man betrayed them? What if they all just died in the desert? He would be abandoning his mama to a life alone.

But if he returned home, he would be leaving Funme and Asilah to fight the Ajungo by themselves.

Unbidden, Lami came to mind. Whether she'd passed on her gift or awoken something in him, he was a Seer now. If she wasn't there to watch over Asilah and Funme, it was his duty. And if this man was telling the truth, maybe Tutu could do more than just protect the cousins. Maybe he could destroy the Ajungo.

There are no heroes in the City of Lies.

"If I do not come?" Tutu asked the Blind Man. "Will you tell me how to find your city? So I can take my people to water."

The Blind Man inclined his head. "Of course."

"And if I come? Why do you need me?"

The man's smile and voice were faint, as if he were lost in memory. "Your mothers tell me you can See."

There are no friends beyond the City of Lies.

"Do you think," Tutu asked after a long pause, "the Ajungo sent those men?"

"Eh?" Asilah raised an eyebrow.

"The men who came to kill me. Who killed Lami. Their leader had a tongue. He must not be from my city. It must be the Ajungo."

Asilah's face became a complex map of emotion that Tutu couldn't read. Funme rubbed his shoulder and kissed his forehead. But neither of them answered him.

"I do not know the answer to your question, young Tutu," the Blind Man finally said, his face turning hard with determination, "but I know where we can find it."

8

TUTU WATCHED FROM atop a high dune as the wagon turned calmly through a valley below, pulled by a team of four camels and encircled by six guards on camels of their own. Its wheels carved deep rivets in the sand, thick enough that the ever-shifting winds couldn't immediately cover them. He recognized those wheel tracks the moment he saw them.

Atop the wagon's wheels lay a clay barrel draped in rich, red cloth. It was massive, large enough for five or six people to stand up inside of it. A young woman sat in the wagon's front seat, one hand on the reins, the other holding a red ball to her lips. She took a bite of it, and Tutu watched in disbelief as she chewed.

"What is that?" he asked.

"Ya don't know wagons?" Asilah asked.

"No, what is she eating?"

"An apple, my Tutu," Funme said. "It is a fruit."

He'd never seen a fruit before. Something about it reminded him of the wood he'd seen in the Palace of Lies. That same wet, breathing quality. A ball of life in a lifeless desert, yet she was just eating it like it was the most common thing in the world.

A bird squawked far to their left.

No, not a bird. When Tutu looked, he saw only a slightly lighter patch in the bronze dunes. He wouldn't have noticed it if he hadn't known exactly where to look. The Blind Man issued another squawk from beneath his desert-colored shroud.

The plan was a simple ambush. The Blind Man would stand in front of the wagon until it came to a halt. Then, Tutu, Asilah, and Funme would slide in and attack from the flank, incapacitating the wagon guards before they had a chance to respond or escape. Then they could interrogate the wagon rider. Tutu hadn't known what that meant, but when he asked Funme, she told him not to worry about it.

It had taken them a week of travel to find the wagon tracks, then another week to catch up to the wagon and scout a position ahead of its crew. Along the way, Asilah and Funme taught Tutu everything they knew about Seeing, telling him stories of Lami's early training and reciting wisdom she'd mentioned over the years.

"Seeing," they told him at the beginning of every training session, "is conviction."

The power came from translating understanding into belief, from standing so firmly in one's knowledge of the world that the knowledge itself became an armor—and a weapon. The more Seers knew, and the stronger their belief in what they knew, the more powerfully they could absorb and channel the energies around them.

Tutu probably now knew more than his entire class combined, including Madam Oda. He knew of an entire world beyond the City of Lies that they couldn't imagine. He didn't have Lami's skill or experience, but by the end of the two weeks, he could easily beat both Asilah and Funme in sparring.

But there was a cost to Seeing. Whatever damage he inflicted, he felt himself. A large part of a Seer's training was numbing oneself to the sensations of the world—to joy and sorrow, anguish and euphoria alike.

"Lami was not always so calm," Asilah had explained. "She was a fiery girl. But as she learned to See, she had to numb herself to protect against the pain."

"All power has a price, young Tutu," Funme warned. "Only give what ya can take."

The Blind Man issued a third and final bird call. Asilah and Funme shifted, readying for violence.

"Be calm, Tutu," Asilah said. She hadn't called him "husband" since Lami's death.

"And stay behind us," Funme added. "Ya only move when the time is right."

Across the sands, the Blind Man emerged from under his shroud. He extended his wooden stick and eased slowly forward until he was standing a few dozen strides ahead of the wagon team.

"Hold!" the wagon driver shouted, shaking the reins until the camels slowed to a halt.

"Out of the way," one of the guards called, trotting toward the Blind Man. "Out of the way, you blind fool."

But the Blind Man didn't move.

"Ready?" Asilah said, looking at Tutu.

He nodded. Not so long ago, the thought of fighting even his classmates had terrified him. Now he was about to attack a convoy of armed men, and he felt as calm as if he were going to buy gari from the market.

"Are you deaf too, you—" the guard began, but the blunt end of the Blind Man's staff took him in the throat. He collapsed to the ground, gasping, and the Blind Man finished him with a blow to the head.

Asilah let out a shrill ululation as her camel sprang forward, charging down the dune and into the valley. She wielded a new, makeshift whip that she'd fashioned out of Bango's leather straps. Funme was just a step behind her, gripping the reins with her remaining hand. Tutu dismounted. Unlike Lami, he needed to be as still as possible to See. Jostling along on the back of a camel was too distracting for him.

As Asilah and Funme cracked their whips at the first two wagon guards, Tutu focused himself. He gathered all he knew and reinforced it with the strength of his belief. Soon, he felt a tingle across every inch of his skin, and the world came into sharper focus, every grain of sand and strand of hair standing out in stark clarity, smells and tastes and textures and emotions as visible to his mind as a desert shadow in broad daylight. His skin began to sparkle.

He found a tangled knot of reality in his Sight, a dense tumor in the back of the wagon that felt more real than everything else around it. Tutu stared at it, entranced and confused.

Shouts between Funme and Asilah snapped his attention back to the task at hand.

"Asi, back!"

"Fufu, on your right!"

After a quick goodbye to Bango, he slid down the slope, iron spear in hand. As the cousins held the center of the battle, Tutu rushed in from the side, where none of the guards had eyes on him. He hurled his spear into the shoulder of one man, ripping him off his mount and impaling him in the sand. The pain hit Tutu immediately, a fire in his own shoulder that immediately convinced him to use less force on the other guards. He jumped onto the back of the next one's camel and delivered a flat hand to the back of the man's neck, slumping him off his mount and onto the sand. Ignoring the dull pain in his own neck, Tutu took the camel's reins and crashed it directly into the camel and rider beside him, leaping free just before impact. As man and beast tumbled to the sand, Funme lashed out with her whip, disarming the guard before he could catch his balance. Tutu followed up with a concussive strike to his chin.

By then, Asilah and the Blind Man had incapacitated the remaining guards in a more lethal manner. Tutu took a moment to breathe out the pain of his strikes.

Then they all turned to the wagon driver.

"Tell us what ya know," Asilah barked, "and ya keep ya head."

The young woman, round-faced and light-skinned with a row of small black balls pierced above the arc of one eyebrow, skated her eyes from Tutu to the cousins to the Blind Man, then over to the one conscious guard writhing in the sand with Tutu's spear protruding from his shoulder.

"I am but a driver," she said, raising her palms, fear on her face. "Transporting my goods. I mean no harm."

Tutu frowned and looked over at Asilah. This wagon was supposed to be a tool of the Ajungo, but this woman looked as confused as Tutu felt.

"Asi!" Funme shouted. She'd made her way to the back of the wagon and raised the cloth draped over the end of the clay barrel. She staggered as she looked into it, as if she'd been struck so hard her legs failed her. Her face was terror. "Come and see," she said, covering her nose with the stump where her hand used to be.

Asilah kept her eyes on the wagon driver as she crept over to Funme's side. She shot a quick glance into the wagon, then froze, eyes locked. "Goddess blind me," she swore.

Tutu hurried over to see what all the worry was about. He rounded the side of the wagon to stare straight into the very mouth of hell.

In a bloody pile, boiled and stinking from the heat, were hundreds of eyes, ears, and tongues. They were a thousand shades of decaying brown, but identical in the jagged violence of their severance, each so stark it was impossible not to imagine the kneeling boy releasing a wordless, gargled scream as his tongue was cut out, or the young girl—as the blade sawed down through her ear—weeping and looking around in desperate terror for any adult to save her.

This was it.

The Ajungo.

Tutu tried to breathe, but each inhale was shallower than the last. A wave of nausea washed over him. And rage. They were equally overwhelming—the venom of disgust and the conflagration of anger; the sad realization of his oppressor's depravity and the deep, welling lust for revenge.

When he looked back at the wagon driver, she was no longer a round-faced innocent. Instead, as she climbed down from her seat and advanced toward them, she was evil itself. "Everything," she sighed, "I must do myself."

Then she took a deep, calming breath that sent a chill down Tutu's spine.

Her skin began to sparkle.

* * *

Asilah's whip lashed out before Tutu could move, but the wagon driver caught it barehanded, tugged forward, and bashed her elbow into Asilah's face. Asilah collapsed in a heap, jaw askew.

"Asi!" Funme shouted, letting her whip fly just as the Blind Man arced his staff at the wagon driver's head.

Both weapons landed but did no damage. The wagon driver absorbed their energy and released it back, bending the air outward in a dome of force that threw both Funme and the Blind Man across the desert.

In a span of seconds, all three were unconscious. Then the wagon rider turned to Tutu.

She was clearly a master Seer. Absorbing energy was an advanced ability, and with the way she had delivered force without contact, she might've been even more skilled than Lami.

But Tutu knew how Seeing worked. As long as he didn't give her anything, he could limit her power. He just needed to keep her from absorbing too much force until he could find an opening to use his biggest advantage: iron.

As if she could read his thoughts, Tutu saw her glance down at the trio of iron daggers strapped to his leather chest piece. He slowly backed away, but the wagon driver stomped her foot, generating energy from the stomp then sending it back to shake the ground beneath Tutu's feet. As he stumbled and fell, she sprang forward, diving atop him with an elbow crashing toward his head.

Tutu rolled out of the way and drew a dagger, but she was already on her feet again. A backhanded blow sent the dagger spinning away and numbed his fingers. He drew his second dagger, but it suffered the same fate. She lunged forward to grab him, but he slipped away and drew his final blade.

"Stop!" he shouted. "Are you Ajungo?"

She froze.

She didn't look much older than him. Maybe driving the wagon was just a job, and she didn't understand who she was working for. Maybe she didn't know what was in the back of the wagon.

"Are . . . are you Ajungo?" he repeated.

She briefly straightened from the crouch of battle, a sneer on her face.

Then she was on him again, swinging punches at his head. He dodged what he could, blocked what he couldn't. He landed a few glancing nicks with his dagger, but only enough to skim lines of red off her skin, never enough to slow her attack. When he raised his forearms to block a barrage of strikes, she tackled him around the waist, driving the air from his lungs and slamming him to the ground. The dagger spun from his grip, losing itself in the sand.

She sat up, looming over him, and threw a heavy fist that he managed to slip at the last moment. Her arm drove into the sand past the elbow. For a moment he just stared, imagining what would have happened to him if her punch had landed. Then he reared back his head and slammed it into her nose.

There was no crunch of bone. No spurt of blood. Only a ringing pain in his skull and a confused, almost disappointed look on the wagon driver's face. She trapped his throat in one hand and raised her fist again. This time, he knew he couldn't slip away.

"Poor boy," she said. "You toy with powers you do not understand."

"Speak for yaself."

Funme took the wagon driver from behind, wrapping one arm around the woman's neck and driving an iron dagger into her ear. She released a gruesome scream, and the sparkle faded from her skin. Then Funme twisted the knife, and the woman collapsed. She moaned in agony as she tried to stem the crimson rush of life pouring from the wound into the sand. Tutu scrambled out from under her.

"You will never find it," she said in a slurred voice, the sand pooling deep red around her.

"These are ya last breaths," Funme replied, blood-drenched dagger in hand. "Speak with care."

"Bury . . ." She tried to crawl away on all fours but stumbled and fell back into a seated position. "Bury me like the rest of it," she finished with barely a voice.

Then she fell face-first into a pool of her own blood, and the last light of life vacated her eyes.

Funme rushed over to check on Asilah, but Tutu couldn't stop staring at the dead wagon rider. He'd seen dead bodies before. He'd seen them his whole life, from the dehydrated corpses being carried through the streets of his city to the guards he'd killed just two weeks before. In the desert, death was a regular yet unwanted visitor.

But the deaths he'd seen as a child were tragedies. Killing the guards had been tragic as well, in a different way. A fight for survival where only one side could win.

This death felt different. It reminded him of his first time in an oasis, which felt so long ago. The way time had slowed and the world around had felt both heavy and infinitely light, like he could float on it and drift away. Freeing.

This death felt good.

Death had always seemed like something that only happened to innocents, but this woman wasn't innocent at all. Nor were her guards. They were guilty, and cruel, and the sight of their bodies sprawled in the sand was as refreshing as a long draught of crisp, cool water.

"Tutu!" Funme called. She held a groggy, groaning Asilah in her arms.

The look she gave him was equal parts angry and concerned, as if he'd snuck out without her permission and returned covered in stab wounds.

He rushed over to help Asilah sit against the wagon and check her injuries. Her jaw was broken, she was missing a tooth, and she was shaking off the effects of concussion, but she didn't seem to have any lasting injuries. The Blind Man had hurt his wrist bracing his fall after the wagon driver's attack, but his injuries were also minor. Not only had they fought and defeated the Ajungo, but they'd done so with minimal consequence. Their last fight had come at a heavy loss; this one had been easy by comparison.

Hours later, however, Asilah couldn't do much more than sit. The blow had damaged her sense of balance, and twice Funme had had to hold Asilah's hair from her face as she vomited. Asilah insisted she was fine, but they kept her seated in the shade against a wagon wheel and allowed her to rest.

"What now?" Tutu asked.

"We were supposed to keep the driver for questioning," the Blind Man said, gingerly touching his damaged wrist.

"So question her," Funme replied. "Ask her why she tried to crush my Tutu's head."

The Blind Man let loose a long sigh. "Did she say anything?"

"One thing," Funme responded. "Bury me like the rest of it."

Asilah snorted. "A waste of words," she said, then groaned in pain and held her jaw.

"Ajungo deserve no burial," the Blind Man added.

Tutu looked up sharply at the large barrel cabin of the wagon. Even without Seeing, he could feel that strange knot sitting in the back of it.

". . . like the rest of it," he mumbled to himself.

"Tutu?" Funme called.

He stood up from beside Asilah and went to the back of the wagon, raising the cloth covering and peering deep into the bloody darkness. He embraced certainty, trusted in his understanding of the world, and used his Sight.

There it was again, buried among the severed tongues and ears and scooped-out eyeballs. Like a grain of sand lodged in the throat—tiny, but impossible to ignore.

He released his Sight.

"It is in here," he said.

"What is?" the Blind Man asked.

"I do not know." Tutu raised one foot up to the lip of the wagon.

"No!" Funme cried. "My Tutu, what are you doing?"

"I . . ." He didn't know. But his body was moving, climbing the back of the wagon and pushing directly into the mangle of body parts.

It was dry. From among the mess, he could see that most of the severed parts were shriveled from the desert heat and splotched with sickly hues of yellow or purple. It was like wading through a sand dune, one with a corrosive stench that scorched the hairs of his nose. But the dryness bothered him more than the smell. These were all parts of human bodies. They should have been living, breathing. Even wood, he'd learned, felt alive. But these parts had been sapped of any life they'd once held. They were dry, dead, no different from a tumbleweed rolling in the wind. There was nothing human about any of it.

And then, as he did so often, he thought of his mama. He wondered if her tongue was among the lifeless flakes, if it was at that very moment getting crushed into dust beneath his feet. The thought of his formidable mama being so inconsequential and expendable made him ooze sweat from every pore. His breathing became a fog of sound that blocked out all others. His heart sprinted. One step took an eternity. His vision began blackening from the edges until there was more darkness than light.

"Tutu!" his mama called from behind him. But he couldn't respond. Couldn't turn to her. He was frozen, breathing harder and louder than he ever had before, struggling to maintain his grip on consciousness.

Then he felt her hands on him, moving him forward where his legs couldn't. Her hands eased his breathing, brought his vision back to clarity. Whatever had been done to his mama, she was there with him now, whole, essential.

When he reached the back wall of the wagon, he bumped his toe against something hard. He held his breath and bent in to the pool of severed parts, closing his hands around a smooth box and pulling it out. He turned to leave the wagon and was surprised to see not his mama but Funme, shoulders hunched to fit her tall frame in the cramped wagon, eyes wide with fear, sweat beading down her cheeks and dripping from her chin.

"Come, my Tutu. Let's go."

Together, leaning on each other, they exited the wagon.

Back in the desert, Tutu took a long breath of fresh, cleansing air, then looked around in confusion.

"I felt her," he said.

Funme didn't ask who. She must have known.

But his mama was nowhere to be found. It had only been his imagination. Of course. He hadn't really believed his mama was there with him. Not really.

All the same, something in his heart turned irreparably bitter with disappointment.

Once Tutu had reclaimed his breath, they all turned their attention to the box in his hands. It was deep black and smooth all around, with no discernible grooves or evidence of what held it all together. And it was light—barely outweighed a feather—but it didn't seem to be hollow. When he held it beside his ear and shook it, he couldn't hear anything jostling within, as if it were a solid brick.

Tutu felt all over it, but there was nothing. No lock, no clasp. No folds, no keyhole.

"What is it?" Funme asked.

Tutu shrugged. "I do not know. But before, with my Sight, I could see it."

"It's the truth," the Blind Man said, making his way over to them. "The answer we didn't know we were looking for."

"Where the wagon is from?" Tutu asked.

"Far bigger than that, young Tutu," he replied. "Inside this box is the answer to who the Ajungo are." He shifted his staff to his left hand and extended his right, palm up. "And I know how to open it."

9

ALL AROUND THEM, the desert was silent. Vultures circled overheard, peering with sharp eyes. Four-legged rodents and hundred-legged insects poked up out of their burrows. Watching.

Waiting.

Tutu held out the black box like he was holding another person's newborn, equal parts care and fear. The Blind Man approached slowly, carrying one of Tutu's daggers. It was the one Funme had used to kill the wagon driver, and its blade was still covered in blood and flesh.

"There is no keyhole," Tutu said. He pounded a fist on the top, but the cube easily absorbed it. It was sturdy. He tried again with his Sight, but surprisingly, the result was the same. "And I cannot break it."

"You need neither key nor force," the Blind Man said. "The only way you were able to find this was by Sight. It is the work of the Goddess. And so . . ."

"Iron," Funme said sadly. Tutu knew that talking about the Goddess or Seeing made her think of Lami. It must have hurt even more to see the Ajungo use the same power that Lami had devoted her life to.

The Blind Man braced the dagger in both hands and leveled it in Tutu's direction. As he pushed it forward, the point touched the black casing, then slid right into it, smooth as a shear through silk. Tutu frowned in disbelief. He didn't know it was possible for metal to part so easily.

Half the blade disappeared into the box before Tutu felt it stick into something too thick to pierce.

"Open it, young Tutu," the Blind Man said as he withdrew the blade.

Tutu dug his fingers into the slit and pried in opposite directions. With surprisingly little force, the box popped evenly into a top and bottom. Between them was a round mass that Tutu couldn't make sense of. He tossed the box's casing aside to inspect its contents.

It was a ball. But unlike the solid black box that had carried it, it wasn't a single piece. Instead, it was made up of endless interlocking tendrils, like something carved from sandstone, but darker in color. And softer.

"What is it?" Tutu asked.

The Blind Man shrugged and turned his head to Funme.

"Wood," she said, eyes narrowed. "A wood ball, I believe. But I do not know this wood."

"This is wood?" Tutu asked, confused. He'd first seen wood in the Palace of Lies. Then he'd seen the Blind Man's staff. Those pieces of wood seemed to live and breathe. This was dead as a statue. It held the idea of life but was empty of the real thing. "It is so dry."

"Ah, the Palm of Ayé," the Blind Man said. "A tree made for the desert. Without water, its roots shrivel into a tight ball. Some say it can live like that forever. But with water, it retakes its true form." He gave a sad smile. "In the old days, many floated down our rivers. Ever since the rivers flooded, we now find them on land like this one. Dry."

"So we need water," Funme said.

Tutu went back to Bango and took a skin from his supplies. He unscrewed the top, then turned it over onto the Palm of Ayé. The water sluiced over the plant, sliding down the hard curves of the inert roots and slipping into the spaces between them. It all immediately soaked in, not a single drop lost to the desert's thirsty sand or evaporating heat.

"And now?" he asked.

"We wait," the Blind Man said.

"For how long?"

Asilah's sudden, sputtering cough drew their attention. She was still seated against the wagon wheel, but now her head hung forward, as if she'd lost all the strength in her neck. Funme rushed to kneel by her side.

"Asi, sit back and . . ."

"What is it?" Tutu asked.

When Funme didn't respond, he moved closer to find strange flecks of red all over Asilah's chin and Funme's hands.

Asilah coughed again, and blood flowed out like sand down an hourglass, rushing down her chest, pooling in Funme's frantic, terrified hands, then spilling more and more and more until their ivory silks were nearly as red as the silks of Oba Ijefi and the court of the Palace of Lies.

And there Asilah died, never learning the truth of the Ajungo.

10

ASILAH'S BODY SHOWED no bites. No broken bones.

They concluded that it must have been the wagon driver's strike that killed her. Tutu couldn't imagine delivering enough force to liquify a person's brain in their skull, but he wasn't half the Seer the wagon driver had been. Funme confirmed that it was possible.

"The power of Seeing is in knowing and believing," she said. "Who can know more than the Ajungo? Who has more reason to believe?"

They buried her in the base of a tall dune.

In the hours it took to bury Asilah, Funme never cried. She never yelled. She never even winced or strained to keep her emotions at bay. She dug through the sand with a workman's effort and efficiency, cut open the torso and removed its organs, laid the body within the hole, and covered it in sand without any ceremony or goodbye. She burned the organs according to custom, staring silently as they turned to ash and scattered in the breeze.

Afterward, she sat by herself away from the wagon, chewing calmly on a strip of dried meat. For a long while, Tutu left her alone. But as time passed and Funme didn't rejoin them, he went over to sit with her.

"Auntie Fufu," he said, extending a skin, "are you thirsty?"

The look she gave Tutu was so bewildered that he raised the skin higher and repeated himself in case she'd heard something he hadn't intended.

"Thirsty?"

Without taking her eyes from his, she grabbed the skin and took a long draught.

"Before we left the city," she said, handing the skin back to him. "Me and Asi worked as runners. In a city where no women can hear, ya can imagine how important letters are. Some days we'd run two, three horizons. But we didn't mind. We were young, strong. We could visit our friends' homes, and sometimes their mamas would give us sweets. I remember one day, we delivered a message to Lami's mama. Lami was just a babe, but she already had so much hair, and it was so soft, like a lamb. So we taught her to mewl like one. '*Mbeeee mbeeee.*' And she would do it, and we would laugh and laugh. That's when we first called her Lami.

"Is this what the Ajungo hate so much?" she asked, wiping drip from her nose and sniffling. "All we want is to be happy. To enjoy those we love. Is this what they work with so much passion to take from us? Can their greed not be satisfied?"

Tutu wasn't sure what to say or do. He rested his head on Funme's shoulder, and she immediately wrapped her arms around him and pulled him in, burying her face in the top of his head.

"Where are your tears, my Tutu?" she said gently. "What have the Ajungo taken from you?"

Tears are precious. Don't waste them on your enemies. Save them for your friends.

Asilah had been his friend. More than that: she'd been family. Lami too. Yet he hadn't cried for either. Maybe he'd used up all his tears by the lake that day. Maybe he had no more left—for neither enemies nor friends.

"Tutu!" the Blind Man called.

Tutu looked over to see the man seated cross-legged in the sand, the Palm of Ayé in his lap.

"What is it?" Tutu asked.

"Come!" he exclaimed. "It's growing."

Tutu helped Funme to her feet, and the two of them hurried over to see the source of the Blind Man's excitement.

The Palm of Ayé was untangling like an intricate knot, each root plumping with life and slithering out of the way of its siblings until it formed the base of the plant—a ring of thick, outward-pointed leaves as bright green as anything Tutu had ever seen. Then the inner core unfurled, revealing a second ring of rounded red flowers that rose in an upward spiral around a central stem. The stem grew, hair by hair, until it was the length of a man's foot. A large, fleshy bulb sat at its tip until it, too, unfurled, its pale petals peeling back.

Within the open flower sat an envelope with a wax seal the color of fresh blood.

Funme grunted. "What is this?"

"Tutu?" the Blind Man asked.

Tutu took the envelope in hand, looked it over. It felt expensive even to the touch, smooth and slick and light in his palm. He broke the seal, lifted up the flap, and slid out a small, folded parchment. It was an off-white that shone faintly pale gold, reflecting the hue of the desert, and it was made of some material Tutu had never seen before.

"Is this a letter?" he asked, both transfixed and chilled to the bone. All that for a letter? What sort of letter was worth swimming through an oasis of body parts for?

He unfolded the paper and looked it over.

It was blank.

He held it up to the sunlight in case some message was written in trick ink.

Blank again.

"There is nothing. Only parchment."

"That is not possible," the Blind Man said, and for the first time since Tutu had met him, Tutu heard an edge of uncertainty in the man's voice. "That . . ."

Funme didn't respond. She just wore a distant, confused look, as if she'd assembled a puzzle but had no idea what the final picture was supposed to be.

There are no heroes in the City of Lies.

No.

He could not fail here. He was a breath away from uncovering the source of all the suffering of the cities of the Forever Desert. Not only that. To become a Seer like the wagon rider, he had to learn more about the world, and there was no bigger secret left than the truth of the Ajungo.

You must learn. He could remember watching his mother sign, the almost imperceptible sound of her fingers flowing from one word to the next. *Only by learning can you free us.*

"There is no water in the City of Lies," he said, suddenly.

Funme and the Blind Man looked at him, one able to see the realization on his face, the other able to sense it.

"That is said in my city," he added. "It has been said for as long as memory."

Funme pursed her lips. "There is no iron in the City of Lies," she added. "That is how we say it."

"To open the box," Tutu said, "we needed iron. To open the Palm of Ayé, we needed water."

The Blind Man let out a low, rolling chuckle. "Young Tutu. Did I not say you were very clever? In my city, we say, 'There are no Eyes in the City of Lies.'"

Tutu took a deep, stabilizing breath and closed his eyes. He imagined his mama. She was the source of everything he knew, the reason for all he believed. He focused on his memory of her— the sad tilt of her eyes, the mirth in her cheeks, the weathered strength of her fingers and all the lessons he had learned from them. From that, he crystallized his understanding of the world and kept it firmly in his heart, held it there until its embers stoked into a warm and cozy fire of conviction.

When he opened his eyes, his skin was sparkling and all the details of the world leapt out at him in a way that only Seers knew. He was unsurprised when he looked down at the letter to find a short message in black ink, written in an orderly script.

> *This writ certifies this wagon as an official carrier for the Free Cities of the Forever Desert. Please dispose of this waste in a secure and discreet manner. Any improper disposal, including any attempt to avoid disposal, will be regarded as an act of treason against the undersigned, punishable by death.*
>
> *Signed,*
> *Oba Ehiz*
> *Oba Abu*
> *Oba Ijefi*

When Tutu finished reading it aloud, he stared at the letter. "I do not understand," he whispered. "Oba Ijefi is my oba."

"And Oba Ehiz mine," the Blind Man said.

"Ours—mine—is Oba Abu," Funme added.

"Then who are the Ajungo?" Tutu asked.

"They named us liars, that we might never trust each other," the Blind Man said, seemingly to himself. "Then they hid the truth behind doors that none of us could open alone. In my city, there are no Eyes to read this letter. In your city, Funme, there is no iron to open the box. And in yours, young Tutu, there is no water to unfurl the Palm of Ayé. They must have believed we would never find this."

"But we did," Funme said. "And they killed us for it."

"They tried. Some of us still stand. And now we know the truth."

"I do not understand," Tutu repeated. He couldn't take his eyes off the letter. Such a short message, written so casually.

They called it waste. The eyes and ears and tongues of thousands of people was just waste. It wasn't being sent to any Ajungo as tribute. It wasn't even being used for some evil ritual. It was just waste to be disposed of. "Oba Ijefi gave me Bango. And weapons. And water. She said she would water my mama for one year. Why would she do this if she is working for the Ajungo? I . . . I do not understand."

"Young Tutu, I thought you were clever," the Blind Man said sharply. "Have you ever seen Ajungo? Have you ever heard the drums of Ajungo soldiers in the distance? Have you ever smelled Ajungo fires on the wind? Of course you understand."

Funme put her arm fully around him, drew him close. "There is no Ajungo," she said gently. "There has never been. Only our own obas. Only us."

In the silence that ensued, Tutu realized that his time in the desert was at an end. The nights spent traveling beneath the bald-faced moon, the delicate days hidden from the sun. The campfire stories and songs at sunrise. Sparring sessions as the jackals watched silently from atop distant dunes. Sleeping like tomorrow was promised, a belly full of water, a head full of dreams.

Because the Blind Man was right. He did understand. He could See everything. He knew the final, terrifying truth of the Forever Desert.

More importantly, he knew in that moment he would never see his mother again. It was a lesson that wrung every drop of hope out of his heart until it was as dry and lifeless as a Palm of Ayé—a stone that was once alive.

You must learn. Only by learning can you free us.

There was nothing left for him to learn.

The only thing left to do was free his city.

11

THE WALLS AROUND the City of Lies hadn't changed in the last eight months. They were as tall as the sky and colorless as the desert, lonely and forlorn against the heat of the world.

There are no friends beyond the City of Lies.

Tutu stood at the foot of the city gates. They'd seen him, he knew. They were just deciding what to do about it. Whereas he had left as a boy with a head nearly bald against the sun, arms and legs sapped of strength, wearing the rough cotton garb of a peasant, he was returning as a man who had seen both life and death, water and blood. His body was strong now, and he wore red silks taken from his enemies, a whip coiled against his right hip, an iron spear strapped across his back, and a crown of black stone beads tight around his head, the curls of his thick hair spilling over its edges.

Though he'd been gone such a short while, he was already a stranger.

The massive double gates groaned as they bent in to welcome him.

He vaguely recognized the woman who stood before him, even with the bronze mask covering the lower half of her face. He'd seen her a lifetime ago in his brief meeting with Oba Ijefi. She was an adviser, maybe. Red-silked guards fanned out behind her, a dozen at least.

Tutu, she signed, her hands moving with a false quiver, as if she were overcome by emotion. *Is that you? Truly?*

He knew she could speak—he knew everything now—but he

allowed her to maintain her charade. "My mama," was all he said.

She ran toward him and wrapped him in a hug that he didn't return. *You must see the oba, Tutu. You have returned!*

The pretense was that she was escorting him to the Palace of Lies, but the way the guards surrounded him in tight columns made it clear they were no honor guard. He was their prisoner.

So they thought.

As they traveled down the wide dust paths he'd grown up on, people staggered out of their shacks, their faces sunken, their skin thin and discolored from dehydration. They stared, unsure of what they were seeing or who this richly garbed man was. This close to the palace, he didn't expect to see any familiar faces, nor did he. His community was farther from the walls, where the water rations were most strict and the people were at their most desperate.

The adviser signed the whole way, telling him how happy everyone would be to see him and how proud he'd made the whole city with his return. Each time he mentioned his mama, she doubled her praise.

They soon arrived at the brown alabaster steps at the foot of the Palace of Lies. As Tutu climbed each step, higher and higher above the city, everything he'd learned in the desert seemed so obviously true that he couldn't believe he had never seen it before. The homes near the palace were larger and nicer than those far away. The people less gaunt. The children less feral and afraid. The land itself was softer, hidden half the day in the shade of the high plateau, free from the scorching desert sun.

How blind he'd been.

Oba Ijefi sat in her throne of red-black wood. The first time he'd seen the throne, he had assumed it was the throne passed down from generations before. From before the Fever. He hadn't even realized how impossible it would have been for wood to survive such dry times. Not wood this healthy, this fresh.

Tutu stood in the center of the throne room, surrounded by Oba Ijefi's court. The people who ruled the City of Lies. The people who had named it, he now knew. Another truth he should have seen before—what other reason was there for them to wear those bronze masks across their lower faces, if not to hide their tongues?

He didn't kneel. Uneasy shifting swept the room until Oba Ijefi finally spoke. "Speaker, you have returned." Her smile was gracious, practiced. "Have you found water?"

"I found many things, my oba," he said as guards emerged from a back room, slipping silently behind the line of Ijefi's royal court. "You see, the desert, in its way, is a school. It taught me that life is filled with lies. There are the shallow lies that can be uncovered by a light wind. And there are the deep lies whose roots extend further down than the eye can see. Lies we don't uproot because we are afraid of the emptiness they will leave behind.

"But I found the truth."

Oba Ijefi adjusted herself in her seat and the soldiers all shared a silent and subtle tensing, readying for combat.

"Where is my mama?" Tutu asked.

"Your mama," the oba said, voice calm as a sleeping city. "I'm sorry, Tutu. We tried everything, but . . . but your mama succumbed to the heat not long ago. If only you had found water. If only you had come home sooner." She narrowed her eyes and her voice fell flat. "You could have saved her."

Even behind her wall of soldiers, Oba Ijefi chose deception. It was all she knew.

His mama—his beautiful, patient, loving, frustrating, wise mama—had been dead for months, killed as soon as he left the city. They must've made up a reason—dehydration or jackals or simply grief from the loss of her son. Any lie that would serve as a bad omen to others, force them to keep their own children from trying to be heroes.

Only by learning can you free us. His mama's words. The first source of truth he'd ever known.

"There are friends beyond the City of Lies," he said, clear and firm. "Many friends, who deserve our trust and generosity. Friends whose love saved my life time and again, and whose bravery will save this world."

The nobles fell back a gasping step and the soldiers stepped forward. They kept their spears upright, but their eyes were ready. Oba Ijefi's mouth hung open the slightest bit, as if she were waiting for the right words to come out.

"There are heroes in the City of Lies," he added, spreading his arms out wide. "There have been many heroes over the years, each of them destroyed, their deeds lost. Many of them were children, slain in the desert before they had a chance to live the lives they deserved. And there would be even more here now, if only they had what they need to be heroic."

The soldiers leveled their spears and took up battle stances, waiting for the command. They were willing to kill for their oba. For this woman and her co-conspirators, who were responsible for the misery of the world. Maybe they didn't know the truth. Maybe they did. Tutu didn't know which was worse.

His skin began to sparkle. He raised a foot and stomped the ground. For a moment, only the thudding sound of his footfall filled the air, but soon there was a deep and yawning groan in the ground beneath them, accompanied by the snaking sound of cracks opening. From his own foot to the foot of Oba Ijefi's throne, a narrow chasm ripped across the room.

Then the floor collapsed inward, folding in on itself and falling away in jagged chunks of black and white. The guards ahead of him screamed in horror as the world fractured beneath them, and their cries for help were met only by the staring disbelief of Oba Ijefi's royal court, her remaining guards peering over the edge of the hole at their doomed comrades.

It was a long silence before the first splash.

Then there was a barrage of splashes, each chunk of floor and terrified guard hushed by a *plunk* and *shoosh*. Tutu looked down into the hole he'd made.

Beneath the Palace of Lies, stored in the plateau atop which it was built, rippled a reservoir of crisp, cool water. Long, thick tree roots spidered across the surface of the water, drinking it in at dozens of points. He traced his eyes along their length up to where they disappeared beneath the crown jewel of the palace: the throne.

"There is water," he said in a near whisper that cut across the silent room, "in the City of Lies."

Oba Ijefi sat in her living tree, stunned. But only for a moment. Then her face twisted into a mask of molten violence, a rage so engulfing that some of her own court stepped away from her.

But Tutu didn't. He hadn't come out of the desert to back down from an oba's tantrum. He took another step forward.

"The one who brings me the Speaker's head will be given five camels and a garden," Oba Ijefi said.

* * *

Every morning after they left the wagon, Tutu would wake and practice Seeing, finding new and creative ways to generate force that he could absorb and unleash. Now that he knew the truth of the Ajungo, he'd never felt so powerful. He'd never felt so certain, so convicted in a belief. He knew he was meant to free his city.

They spent another two weeks together, refilling their water, replenishing supplies, living off the land. Tutu spent every free moment training to fight as a Seer. Funme and the Blind Man didn't train with him. The Blind Man spent that time sleeping or weaving himself a new cloak. Funme just watched Tutu from a distance, a concern on her face that she seemed scared to voice.

Over those two weeks, they spoke often about what to do with their new knowledge, how they could break the centuries-old tyranny of the obas of the Forever Desert. Or at least Funme and the Blind Man spoke. Tutu sat silently as they did, refusing to participate. They didn't understand. They couldn't See what he saw.

Finally, they parted ways. The Blind Man left first, heading northeast to return to his city.

"Come with me, young Tutu," he said. "In my city, I have the support of the people. With your mind and your Sight, we can free my city and bring its waters to yours."

Tutu ignored the request. He already had a plan of his own. He didn't need the Blind Man's water anymore. "What is your name?" he asked.

"Me?" the Blind Man asked. "I am called Ogoro."

"Ogoro," Tutu said, tasting the word. He didn't have any reason for knowing the man's name. He didn't like him or trust him. He just wanted to know. Knowing was everything.

He took Ogoro's forearm in his hand and shook it. "Go in peace."

"Go in peace," Ogoro said with an uncertain smile.

After a brief hug and goodbye to Funme, Ogoro mounted his camel and rode into the desert.

Then it was time to say goodbye to Funme.

They hugged for a long time, neither saying anything, just appreciating the safety they brought to each other's lives.

"Ya can come with me," Funme said. "Ya know iron. There are some who are ready to fight. But we are few. We can use ya help, my Tutu, to free our city."

He was tempted. The desert was a lonely place, and he had grown so comfortable traveling with her that he was already beginning to feel that discomfort in his gut, the fear of the unfamiliar.

But he already had a plan of his own. He didn't need Funme's companionship anymore. He didn't need anyone but himself.

"Go in peace, Auntie Fufu," he said.

She pulled back from their embrace, took his face in her hands, and gave him a long, searching look. "My Tutu: my boy who became a man. I see this. But a man needs help as well. A man needs friends. I can come with ya, and when we free ya city, we can free my own. For Lami. For Asilah. We will be everything the Ajungo fear."

He realized that she was more scared than he was. Adults were always scared. They hid it in a million ways—caution or confidence, disinterest or anger, a firm hand or warm embrace or sage advice—but the fear was always there if you knew how to see it.

But Tutu had experienced all his fear as a child. Death, abandonment, failure, loneliness—he'd been forced to confront all of them by the age of thirteen, and all it had done was help him See more clearly. Now, there was no fear left in him.

He didn't want help.

He didn't want friends.

He didn't even want freedom. Not anymore.

"I love you, Auntie Fufu," he said.

Funme stiffened, eyes locked on his. Then she melted into him, burying her face in his shoulder. As she enveloped him in her long arms, he could feel the weight of her, the heaviness she was taking back to her city.

"My son," she whispered in his ear, and she felt so much like his mama that for a moment he thought he was back home, kneeling in their cramped hut before heading out to school. "Go in peace."

She meant it when she said it. That was why he had refused to go with them, or to allow them to come with him.

He didn't want peace.

*　　*　　*

The guards, those few who had avoided plummeting into the water below, were dead before they could move. Tutu had figured out the wagon driver's trick of releasing her energy as a shockwave, and he had even improved on it. He took force from his stomp and sent out seven concentrated bolts, one for the throat of each guard. The guards crumpled as their windpipes crushed, some clawing at their throats, others falling immediately unconscious from the trauma, slipping quietly into death.

And Tutu felt none of it. From within his Sight, he should have suffered their same pain, felt the crush of his own throat seven times over. But he'd spent his time in the desert wisely. He'd successfully numbed himself to the pain of his enemies.

The oba's court devolved into madness, each of them screaming and fleeing, escaping down staircases and into back rooms.

Oba Ijefi, however, didn't move.

"Seers!" she shrieked.

Immediately, Tutu could feel their presence as they used their Sight. Three Seers—each at least as strong as the wagon driver, he knew—took up positions around him and approached slowly. A fourth came from behind, closing off any chance of escape.

They seemed to think he would try to escape. They still didn't understand why he was there.

The first Seer threw a quick blur of strikes, but Tutu parried each one and responded with a strike to her chest that hit past skin and muscle and bone and stopped the heart itself.

Before she collapsed, he had already rounded on the others. They came fast, in a coordinated weave of attacks, some directed at Tutu and some directed at each other, transferring energy faster than Tutu could track. He thought they'd pooled their energy into one, but that Seer's punch landed lightly, only for another to send him hurtling across the room and crashing into a far wall.

But even together, they were too weak.

He climbed back to his feet and dusted himself off. Then he walked calmly toward them and played their game, parrying each attack and watching, waiting for the opening.

When it came—when the Seer who'd accepted all their energy launched a kick at his head—he was ready. He absorbed the superpowered impact of the shin against his skull, and used it for his own. He caught the kick in one arm and brought his other arm down, exploding through the Seer's knee like an axe through chicken bone. He hit the next Seer with three rapid punches that pushed ribs through lungs, and he headbutted the final Seer the way Lami had headbutted the desert creature so long ago, meeting force with force and trusting that his was greater. The Seer's eyes burst from the impact, and she dropped to the ground, skull blown open at the back.

He turned to Oba Ijefi then, and through the cold rage in his heart, he almost enjoyed the disbelief on her face. Those were probably four of the strongest Seers in the Forever Desert, and he'd disposed of them as effortlessly as the obas of the Forever Desert had disposed of so many eyes, ears, and tongues throughout the centuries.

He knew she didn't understand. Seeing was about conviction. The better you understood the world and the more fully you believed it, the more powerfully you could See.

None of the elites of the three Cities of Lies really understood the world. They knew the big secret, of course. They knew that all of history was a lie told to instill fear in those whose fearlessness could have rewritten it. They knew the only Ajungo were themselves. They knew power.

But they didn't know powerlessness. They didn't know what

it meant to have your gods stolen from you, leaving you blind to your own past. They didn't know what it was to be deprived of iron, waiting helplessly for monsters to come ruin everything you loved. They didn't know how it felt to live in a world with no friends, no heroes. A world of never-ending thirst.

And their ignorance made them weak.

Auntie Fufu said that all power had a price. He wished she could've been there to see Oba Ijefi's face. Her and Lami and Asilah. The oba's face was the opposite of conviction, the realization that maybe everything she knew to be true wasn't true at all.

"Please," she said.

Tutu stared.

"Please, Speaker. I am your oba, please. Whatever you desire, I can give to you. Anything. *Every*thing. Spare me, Speaker."

He almost laughed. Instead, he made a simple statement: "You killed my mama."

Suddenly, he was a boy again. He was unprepared for the stinging rush of tears that sprang to his eyes. For the quiver in his lips and hands. For the rapid breathing and dizzying swirl of his head. For the heartrending realization that he'd learned more than anyone else alive and it meant nothing—he hadn't saved the only person who mattered to him.

He rubbed his shaking wrist across his face to wipe the tears away. Not because he was ashamed of them, but because the oba was watching and they weren't hers to see.

Don't waste them on your enemies.

"You killed my mama," he said again with a steady, adult voice.

Then he hurled his spear forward, sending it whistling through the air. Oba Ijefi didn't even have time to throw up her arms. Her only reaction was a slight widening of the eyes. Tutu had seen many deaths, and for most people, there was a look of understanding at the end, as they came to realize how much they'd overestimated their own durability. He'd seen it in the Vulture, in the wagon driver. In Lami. But for Oba Ijefi, her disbelief only grew, and as the spear tore through her gut—shearing through organ and muscle and bone, driving even through the thick wooden throne behind her, and splitting with a great, cracking boom the back wall of the Palace of Lies—she died with even less understanding than she'd lived.

Fissures radiated out from the point of the spear, fracturing the back wall until it burst into a cloud of collapsing debris. As that wall fell, it tore the others down with it, bringing the whole Palace of Lies crumbling down until, after the dust settled, the sun shone across the checkered floor. A rumble from the base of the mountain drew Tutu over to the far side of the room to look out over the City of Lies.

Below him, water was forcing its way out from a crack, first in angry spurts, then in a steady gush. Soon, a flood burst forth from the mountain, rolling down its craggy back and into the city below. The flood demolished the buildings near the Palace— the homes and minor palaces of Oba Ijefi's court. By the time it reached the poorest neighborhoods in the heart of the city, it was an ankle-high blessing. He watched with pride and relief and a throbbing, aching heart as the sand beneath his old neighborhood soaked dark with water. The sand in which his mama was most likely buried.

Tutu was watching the stolen water return to its people when the guard's spear rammed up through his back, its iron tip tearing through his ribcage. A final act of bravery from a man with a broken throat, willing to die for an already-dead oba who probably hadn't even known his name.

Tutu didn't turn to face the man. He didn't try to remove the spear or stem the flow of blood. He didn't scream for help.

He kept his eyes on the gushing water as it settled into a natural valley across the center of the city, where a river must have flowed many ages ago and would now flow again. He watched it for as long as he could until his legs gave out. Even then, face against the ground, he kept his eyes on the spreading water as his own blood pooled atop the black-and-white palace floor.

As his life ended, Tutu thought about the empty mountain below him and how it was up to the people of the now-nameless city to fill it with something better. He thought about Ogoro and Funme, hoping their own cities would have the same opportunity. He thought about the story that would be told of this day and whether, when history was written, he would be the hero who ushered in the new world or the villain who destroyed the old one.

He saved his final thoughts for his mama.

Tutu had made her a twofold promise: to find water and to return to her. As his vision darkened toward death, he saw in the distance the house they'd lived in, now sitting upon watered land. He imagined that water soaking deep into the ground, to his mama's body buried in the sand, dripping onto her lips. He'd fulfilled the promise of water.

Then, with the last of his energy, Tutu closed his eyes and fulfilled his promise to return.

ACKNOWLEDGMENTS

I'm a child of immigrants, which means I live in two realities. Each is fully real and true and worthy of pride. And in both realities, I'm an outsider, neither at home in Nigerian culture nor American. There is pain in feeling excluded, of course, but there's also power—it's easier to see the forest fire from outside the forest than from within. But I'd never been comfortable speaking from my outside perspective.

That was until I wrote that opening line—"There is no water in the City of Lies." That perfect phrase—that perfect truth and perfect lie—was exactly what I wanted to say. And I realized I couldn't stop writing until I'd poured out every bit of my truth into this city I'd birthed, and hoped that truth would make sense to others.

Speaking of others.

This book wouldn't exist without my editor, Carl Engle-Laird, who approached me at a reading years ago and told me he liked my writing, even though I myself didn't yet know what "my" writing actually was. It was the first time anyone "in the industry" expressed interest in me, and it gave me the confidence to push forward. Working with him and editorial assistant Matt Rusin has been a dream, truly, and I can't thank them enough for the freedom they've given me to tell my truth.

Speaking of dreams, it's still surreal to me that Jim McCarthy is my agent, but he's the best and is so willing to share his immense industry wisdom. It's also surreal that Irene Gallo is my publisher. Irene doesn't know how much of a fanboy I am of hers (guess she's finding out now), but the day she followed me on

Twitter was one of the most incredible, eyes-brimming-with-tears-emoji days of my life. Her creative vision is immense, and she's an artist in a way I can only someday hope to be.

Thanks to Alyssa Winans, who took my vague *"Attack on Titan in North Africa vibez"* cover pitch and crafted a work of art that I am so proud to share with the world. And to Christine Foltzer for a full cover design that has made everyone I've shown it to immediately go "oh wow." Thanks to my managing editor, Lauren Hougen, and production editor, Dakota Griffin. Thanks to production manager Jackie Huber-Rodriguez. To the marketing team, Julia Bergen, Michael Dudding, Sam Friedlander, and Kaleb Russell, for helping a man who truly sucks at marketing (me) reach an audience he would otherwise be clueless at reaching. To publicist Alexis Saarela for helping a man who truly sucks at publicity (me) present himself like an actual adult to people who would be willing to read this book. Thanks to copyeditor Michelle Li and proofreader Sara Thwaite. I'm a man who makes a lot of errors and is horrible at sticking to self-created style guides. Thank you for making this book coherent.

Thanks to the friends who helped make this book possible. Thanks to Sarah al-Tamimi, whose deep emotional understanding of the work convinced me that I was on to something. To Cade Hagen, my forever writing bro, who helped me patch up a number of early plot holes. To my writing group members—Woody, Ananda, Nick, Alyssa, Cooper, Jon, Griffith—for looking over the messy first draft of this and helping me better understand this story's position on the intersection between fable and fantasy.

Lastly, thanks to you all, the readers. Some of you are friends and family who are reading to support me. Some of you are reviewers or other industry professionals who are obligated to read it. Most of you, I hope, are just strangers who picked it up because they were told it would offer them something they wanted—a good yarn or thought-provoking themes or characters they could root for and see themselves in. This book was written as a fever dream, and the fact that you're all willing to share that dream with me means a lot. It means the world. I'm indebted to each and every one of you; I hope the next two books pay that debt.